CIRCLE OF DEATH

Japanese soldiers stood in a circle around Mc-Leane. With his hands tied behind his back he seemed like dead meat. Shrilly, one of the Japs yelled something at him. McLeane ignored the soldier and scanned the darkness. At ten o'clock, a few yards away, he saw an opening in the jungle undergrowth.

Slowly, quietly, he worked his hands. He might loosen the rope that bound them, but that would take time. He had no idea what the noble son of Hirohito standing in front of him was thinking, however he suspected that sooner or later his Oriental hosts would put a bullet through his brain. He also wondered how long it would be before he found out whether or not they intended to pull out his toenails first.

McLEANE'S RANGERS #4

RANGERS

SAIPAN SLAUGHTER

BY JOHN DARBY

ZEBRA BOOKS

KENSINGTON PUBLISHING CORP.

ZEBRA BOOKS

are published by

Kensington Publishing Corp.
475 Park Avenue South
New York, NY 10016

First printing: January 1985

Printed in the United States of America

Chapter One

On any map of the world the Marianas look like a line of insects running north to south in the Pacific, somewhat to the east of the Philippines. They yield no important resources and offer tourists no wild night life. There is nothing much to see on them. Why anyone would even want to visit these tiny, hilly rocks carved into caves, much less fight for them, defies the imagination. But fight for them the Allies did, very hard, in one of the great battles of the Second World War.

By the spring of 1944 the Allies had grown tired of the war, and they were frustrated by the Japanese resistance. Against overwhelming odds, superior weaponry, and more highly trained personnel, the sons of Hirohito managed to hang on—and to strike decisively when the Australians and Americans least expected them to do so. In a final effort to end the conflict in the Pacific the Allied Command decided to move against the southern Marianas: Guam, Saipan, and Tinian. The navy wanted the islands as logistical bases, the army air force for landing strips. The Allied Command also decided that the Rangers had to knock out the enemy headquarters and the thick pockets of resistance on Saipan before their offensive would work.

Archibald Thompson, General, United States Marine Corps, broke the news to McLeane over coffee in the unit canteen on Vella la Vella.

"This is an extremely important mission, Mac, and extremely dangerous."

"As opposed to the last mission, which was unimportant and a piece of cake." McLeane could not resist the dig.

"We've decided you're the only one who can do this."

McLeane sat silent and motionless.

"Saipan is riddled with Jap guerrilla units," Thompson went on. "They've holed up in caves in threes and fives. These are the emperor's best. They don't give up. They're going to die on that island. They're also well equipped."

"That's all right, Arch. Don't mince words. Give it to me straight."

Thompson smiled.

The coffee had gone cold. Just once McLeane wanted to meet the guys who came up with these bright ideas. He at least wanted to know their names. But William McLeane, Major, United States Marines, never asked questions.

"Can I get you a fresh cup of coffee, Mac?"

"No, that's OK. Nothing else is right. Why should the coffee be good?"

"I know how you feel."

McLeane doubted that. He doubted that a lot.

"I know the men still hurt from blowing Hill 457."

Actually, on that score the Rangers had come out pretty well, McLeane reflected. His own left shoulder would always be stiff from the bayonet wound, but he had already gotten used to the slower movement and to the slight ache that went all the way to his fingers every time he lifted his arm. Heinman and O'Connor had come out in one piece. By some miracle Wilkins's leg had healed, though with no help from Wilkins who'd insisted on getting out of bed every five minutes to walk around.

Contardo had become McLeane's real problem. Unless the wiry little Italian from Flatbush could tear off somebody's upper lip twice a week he would develop all the symptoms of deep depression. Yesterday, McLeane had found him sitting alone, far from camp, under a banyan tree, ripping a three-week-old *Stars and Stripes* into little pieces, and muttering. The exact theme of these mutterings escaped McLeane. He remembered only the overloud use of *fucker* every third word. In fact, in a little while, all the Rangers would be muttering and using fucker every third word.

But then the Rangers always did prefer war to peace. On balance McLeane thought "the fearsome foursome," as they called themselves, would be better off fighting someone else than each other. And if they did not fight someone else soon, they would be

7

fighting each other. Just the thought of them bickering made McLeane want to take on the entire Jap army.

"What do we have to do?"

McLeane lit another Chesterfield. The dark tent felt close around him. The Rangers would do whatever they had to do.

"Mac, I'm about to tell you something in strictest confidence."

Thompson put on his in-strictest-confidence face. The sour expression matched his crew cut and nervous stomach. McLeane always found the good general more believable when he frowned. He never trusted a general who was smiling. McLeane sat comfortably across from the man who had been his commanding officer during the time he'd spent in the Pacific. He waited.

"We're planning a major offensive against the southern Marianas on June fifteenth. We're throwing everything we can at them—planes, ships, men. This could be our biggest move of the war."

This information came as news to McLeane.

"But, as you know, the Marianas are tough."

This information did not come as news to McLeane.

McLeane said nothing. He took Thompson's cup, walked slowly to the oversize canister, and poured two coffees. He could see the Pacific dawn, bright and white, through the canteen entrance. He wondered when he'd last had a good night's sleep and he wondered if he would ever have one again.

"There's a report I want you to read," Thompson said, cupping his coffee in both hands.

"Intelligence?"

"Now, I know how you feel about Major Flagg."

"I'll read it, General."

"I was under the impression . . ."

"I said I would read it. Really, I will read it."

"After he was such a big help with Hill 457, I figured you two . . ."

"Please let me have the report . . . sir."

If McLeane didn't exactly hate Flagg anymore, he didn't exactly like him either. But what the hell!

"It's back in my quarters. I'll get it to you before afternoon mess."

"Thanks. Anything else?"

"Nope. I'll go out with you."

The two men paused outside in the fresh air. Ahead of them lay nothing but the blue Pacific. Thompson took a deep breath.

"Great." He took another deep breath. "Isn't that great? Feel the air rush into your lungs. Try it. Breathe deeply. Go on."

Thompson exaggerated his chest and sucked in half the atmosphere around Vella la Vella. McLeane tried to do the same thing.

"Isn't that great?"

"May I say something, sir?"

"You always do anyway."

"You drink too much coffee and don't get enough rest."

Thompson actually laughed. He took McLeane's hand. "Major, I'm glad you're the only guys in the phone book under 'Rangers'."

*   *   *

McLeane entered the quarters he shared with Margot Thomas, Private, United States Marine Corps. She stood with her back to the entrance, toweling a radiant head of thick, red hair. He came up quietly behind her and, reaching around, gently cupped her ample breasts which jutted, warm and free, under a loose-fitting fatigue shirt.

"O.K., lady, give me everything you've got," McLeane whispered, his mouth against her ear.

Margot didn't flinch.

"You've already got everything I've got."

He nuzzled her neck.

"Then tell me where the Rangers are going on their next mission."

"What makes you think I know?"

She wrapped the towel around her hair.

"Because you run the radio on this island, lady. You know everything." He softly kneaded her breasts.

"What's in it for me?"

McLeane pushed an ever-growing erection against her back.

"You're going to Saipan."

McLeane did not let up.

"What else do I want to know about my mission, lady?"

Her breath came heavily. He kissed her neck as she laid her head back. He could hear her purr.

"Why are you doing this to me, Mac?"

"Tell me everything I want to know or I'll stop."

"Stop it," Margot said not wanting him to stop it. "Please . . ."

"I do, and you'll die."

Her body began to move ever so slightly in a

familiar rhythm.

"Please . . ."

McLeane was pleased with himself. He could feel her body surrender completely.

"Well, I can tell you one thing, Major McLeane."

"Do, yes."

"You're going by sub."

"How nice to be beneath the sea with all the fishes." He began to unbutton her shirt, to move his hand down over her belly.

"Do you always walk around in panties, lady?"

She opened her legs.

"Only when I know you'll come by."

He carried her to the cot on which they both had lain only hours before and deftly removed her shirt, then her panties.

"Oh, my God, Mac," she groaned. "Hurry."

She opened her eyes to see him standing naked in front of her. His massive chest and strong arms took her breath away. She noticed once again that his body tapered into a V at the waist, that his stomach muscles rippled, that his thighs were massive. She wanted him desperately, spread herself wide in offering.

He entered her at once.

"Oh, my God! Oh, my God!" She could not stifle her own cries of joy.

McLeane said nothing, but rode her easily, steadily, hard.

"I love you, Mac. I love you. I love you. I love you." The words became a chant as her body moved to meet his, moved to a music they alone heard.

As the tempo quickened, Margot's need became more urgent and she shook her head, tossing that glorious mane of thick, red hair from side to side.

"Oh, I love you so much, Mac." Her voice was breathy and hoarse. "I'll do anything for you, anything, anything . . . anything."

On the verge of exploding, she could no longer speak, but threw her legs around his back and pulled him close. McLeane played her like a master. At just the right moment he withdrew.

"Oh, no, Mac, please, no . . . no, please."

Then he entered her again hard and the world turned all the colors of the rainbow and for the briefest moment she thought she would black out . . . had blacked out . . . as wave after wave of ecstasy rolled up and down her spine and through her limbs.

Margot clung tightly to McLeane long after they'd both stopped moving. She took time to regain her breath, to speak.

"You are magnificent," she said finally, between gasps. "I can't remember feeling like that since . . ."

McLeane looked at his watch.

"Since about four and a half hours ago." He finished the sentence for her.

"Has it only been that long?"

"Time doesn't lie."

She snuggled close to him, buried her head in his massive chest, took his leg between her thighs.

"I love you so much, Major William McLeane."

McLeane wanted to smoke. He also had strong feelings for Margot, whatever they were, but at that exact moment he wanted a Chesterfield, more than anything. As gently, diplomatically as possible, he disengaged himself from her body and, in what he hoped would be regarded as a perfectly usual, casual gesture, lit up.

12

They shared the bed in silence. McLeane heard her sigh.

"What kind of sub?" he asked.

"Huh?" She looked up startled, half asleep.

"You said we were going by sub, and I asked what kind of sub."

Her head dropped.

"You're so romantic."

"And what happened to Corrigan?"

"Someone named McKendrick wanted him."

McLeane smiled. Colonel P. J. McKendrick of the Australian Royal Navy ran commando operations for the Aussies in the Pacific. He also drank with Bramley and the rest of the Allied Command. Corrigan had moved up in the world.

"What did he want him for, Redbird, my beauty?"

"Don't know." Redbird spoke softly with her mouth against McLeane's ear. She began to move, slowly at first, up and down against his leg. Her tongue shot out, and she kissed his neck. McLeane pretended not to notice. She placed a gentle hand between his legs.

"Make love to me, Mac."

She stroked him.

"Make love to me, Mac."

McLeane looked at his watch and rolled over toward Margot's lush body. He had never ever been inside a submarine. His passion rose.

McLeane ground out a freshly lit Chesterfield in the empty C-Ration tin that served as an ashtray. He looked down for a moment at the sheaf of papers on his lap; then he flung it across the tent. The front page, marked Top Secret, landed face up on the table Margot used to make coffee.

"What's wrong, darling?" Margot looked up from a newly brewed pot.

McLeane climbed slowly out of the cot on which he and Margot had spent most of the last six hours. Every muscle on his chest and arms stood out taut and angry. He said nothing.

"Are you all right?" Margot touched him lightly on the hand. "Talk to me?"

McLeane put on his shirt and pants without a word. She could feel him breathing hard.

"Flagg's report." He pointed in the direction of the strewn papers. "Great work! The Japs have a guerrilla headquarters somewhere in the middle of Saipan, but intelligence doesn't know exactly where. In fact, it moves around a lot and at this very minute it could be at the northernmost tip of Guam or of southern Tinian, for that matter.

"This headquarters has anywhere from five to one hundred fifty men, all of them either fierce warriors or total incompetents. They are either the best equipped troops in the Pacific or are out there with bows and arrows. On page one they are holed up in a heavily guarded fort. On page five they live in scattered caves.

"Now this is just the kind of good hard info we need to get our asses shot off. Doesn't Thompson read this crap?"

McLeane stormed out of the tent into the balmy tropical afternoon. Margot knew better than to go after him. She would calm him down before he left on the mission.

14

Chapter Two

Cpl. Vince Contardo lay on his back in the top berth of a small compartment he shared with three other Rangers aboard the submarine U.S.S. Mako. He stared at the pipes inches away from his nose and wondered where they went and why, and what any of them had to do with him.

"Don't give your nose much room, does it?"

The voice of the usually silent Wilkins floated across to him. Reaching over, he could almost have touched his bunk.

"Leave my fucking nose out of this mission." Contardo found himself, unconsciously, touching the very tip of it.

"Ain't no reason to be touchy, Vince. My nose ain't near as big as yours, and I can't breathe neither."

After the vast outdoors of Vella la Vella, Contardo found himself, in fact most of the Rangers found themselves, climbing the walls. No one smoked in the close air.

"Where the fuck are we going?" Finally, Contardo had to say something even though talking used up oxygen.

No one answered.

"I asked where the fuck we're going? You guys dead?"

"We're going to the Marianas." Heinman said flatly from the berth below Wilkins.

"I know that, asshole. I want to know if we're going north or east, in what fucking direction we're going." Inside the sub Contardo had lost all sense of the compass and without such a bearing he became very nervous.

"North."

Heinman knew everything.

"North. Just north? What kind of fucking answer is that: 'North'? North what?"

"North is good enough for now. When it changes, I'll let you know. Keep tuned to this station."

"Such a fucking smartass . . . Knows everything."

Heinman understood the edge in Contardo's voice. After only a few hours, the confinement had worked on Contardo's nerves. By the time the Rangers hit Saipan Contardo would be ready to take on every Jap soldier in the Pacific as well as the entire Imperial Navy single-handed. Heinman smiled.

"Now, you know in the woods, the bears—"

Contardo cut Wilkins short.

"We ain't in no woods, with no fucking bears, you dumb shit. We're in the ocean with the fucking fish. So don't talk to me about the fucking woods."

After a moment, Wilkins tried again.

"I only meant—"

"I don't give a shit what you meant, hillbilly. It don't apply under the water."

Contardo waited a long time to ask a question that had been bothering him ever since he'd come on board.

"How far down are we, Heinman?"

Heinman didn't say a word. He'd decided to let Contardo sweat it out.

"Hey, Heinman? How far down are we?"

"How far do you think?"

"I don't think. Just give me a fucking answer."

"How's thirty thousand feet sound—"

Contardo banged his head jumping out of his berth.

"Thirty thousand feet?"

"Too much? Too little?"

"Come on, Heinman. Don't play games. This is serious shit." He settled down to await the truth.

"Try three hundred feet."

"Throughout his entire conversation with Contardo Heinman had been reading a *National Geographic* devoted entirely to the Ibo of Southeast Nigeria.

"What do you mean 'Try three hundred feet'? Is it three hundred feet?"

"About that."

Contardo, Heinman knew, did not feel comfortable with this topic, and did not feel easy under water.

Wilkins lay quietly, looking up at the bulkhead only inches from his face. He could hear Contardo fidget and Heinman turn pages.

"You related to the Ibo, Contardo?" Heinman

17

called up from below.

"What the fuck's that supposed to mean?"

"Just wondering."

McLeane walked in on a lull. Everything seemed unusually quiet.

"Hello, sir."

"Hello, Heinman."

Wilkins and Contardo both just looked down from above and nodded. Then, McLeane saw O'Connor, underneath Contardo. On his side, eyes half closed, he was breathing through his mouth, his face a pale gray-green.

"You all right, O'Connor?"

"If you will forgive me, sir, he's seasick," Heinman volunteered because O'Connor couldn't talk. He only gave a faint nod and stuck the flat of his tongue out of his mouth. Contardo hung his head over the bunk.

"Keep an eye on him will you, Heinman?" McLeane turned to leave. "Take it easy, men."

"Take it easy, sir." All of them, except O'Connor replied, if not in unison, at least sincerely. McLeane had no sooner stepped outside the compartment than he heard Contardo's voice.

"Hey, O'Connor, you dumb Irish fuck. How about a nice pastrami sandwich on rye with lots of mustard and pickles, and caraway seeds in the rye and lots of fat on the pastrami."

McLeane hoped they would run into some Japs soon.

Lieutenant Commander C. K. Henderson ran a

tight submarine. The Mako had been commissioned by the Navy only the year before, looked like new; and Henderson intended to keep her looking that way. He and McLeane sat together in the captain's quarters drinking malt Scotch from canteen cups.

"I've heard about you, McLeane." Henderson had a weather-beaten face and gnarled fingers, and he had a voice like a foghorn. "You guys really know how to kick ass."

McLeane just nodded. He had, sadly, never heard of C. K. Henderson or the Mako before yesterday.

"Yep, you guys must be something else. Frankly, I don't know how you do it?"

McLeane looked a little bewildered.

"I mean I don't know how you do all those things you do."

"We just do them, Commander." McLeane had absolutely no idea what this man was talking about.

"Look, Major, let's face it. You guys don't look like much."

Suddenly, McLeane understood Commander Henderson.

"How so, Commander?"

"Besides yourself, the only other one of you guys bigger than a Jap is laid up, seasick. One guy wears glasses. Another guy isn't old enough to shave. And that skinny little guy with the big nose I could break in half like a match stick."

McLeane just nodded his head. Henderson poured another three fingers each of Scotch. McLeane didn't want it, but he said nothing.

"Come on, drink it down." Henderson looked at McLeane and took a long slug. McLeane sipped his.

19

Henderson poured himself another.

"No, sir, Major, I don't see how you guys did any of the stuff you're supposed to have done.

He looked down at McLeane. McLeane stood up.

"I think I had better get back to my men."

A lieutenant commander in the Navy holds the same rank as a major in the Marine Corps, but McLeane wanted to avoid an incident. Henderson, after all, did command the sub.

"No, Major, sit down. You've got nowhere to go on a submarine. On one of them big battleships maybe you can go on board and look out on the ocean, but not on one of these things. No, I'm afraid that this is the most fun you're going to have until you hit Saipan."

McLeane suppressed an urge to put Henderson through the bulkhead. Instead he sat down and concentrated on the lines on his face. He thought of a road map. Before him McLeane saw a tough, bitter old tar who had probably been passed over for promotion many times.

Suddenly a horn signaled three times. McLeane looked up.

"Mess horn. Don't worry, I sent somebody to get your guys to eat. They oughta like it. We got good food."

The Navy always ate well. Besides, anything had to be better than what passed for meals on Vella la Vella.

"Sorry if I got offensive a few minutes ago. I didn't mean it."

The two men sat for a time in silence. Then Henderson showed McLeane his navigator's map, pointed out the exact latitude and longitude of their present position, and demonstrated how to calculate fuel supply, all of which McLeane knew anyway, being a Marine.

How quickly they forget we're part of the Navy, McLeane thought.

The commander's explanation of torpedoing, however, completely engrossed McLeane. Henderson gave a mock demonstration of how a periscope works and calculated how to send a torpedo on target. Then the commander had poured himself another stiff shot and sat back in his captain's chair.

"So tell me how it is with you guys." He handed McLeane a Chesterfield.

McLeane did not know what to say.

"We do our job."

"Yeah, but how?" He hesitated. "You got nothing but a bunch of fairies."

McLeane let his anger pass; then he answered in a measured voice.

"Let's take the four-eyed fairy first, Commander. That's Heinman. Fairy Heinman studied at Oxford, holds a doctorate in Oriental studies, speaks quite a few languages—including a few Pacific dialects. He also happens to be the best martial arts expert I, personally, have ever seen, maybe the best martial arts expert anyone has ever seen.

"Let's also take the seasick fairy, O'Connor. Where do you live, Commander?"

"What's that have to do with anything?"

"Please."

"Indianapolis. Just outside Indianapolis. You wouldn't like a shot?"

"No, Commander, thank you. Indianapolis is fine." McLeane had a hard time keeping the smirk off his face. "O'Connor could blow up all of downtown Indianapolis with a bomb the size of a dime, or if you want something more subtle, Commander, he could blow a dime off the end of your dick and you wouldn't know the difference, except for a slight burning sensation. Sorry to be so graphic."

He had seen the commander wince.

"Otherwise, O'Connor would just as easily club your brains into the ground. He has fists like hams, is built like a bull, and does not believe in boxing."

McLeane doubted his rundown had made any impression on Henderson. He, however, had enjoyed it immensely. He had lived over two years with all four of these men, knew them better than he knew himself, and would have thrown himself under a train for any one of them.

"Now, as for the fairy who isn't old enough to shave, Wilkins, he's the only marksman I know who could shoot O'Connor's charge off the end of your dick without you knowing it."

McLeane seldom used such crude analogies, but with Henderson he felt they were apt. Already the Commander had had too much Scotch.

"Finally, we have the skinny one with the big nose." McLeane got up. "I will only say this, Commander: if Contardo ever knew that you had even thought of calling him a fairy, you would disappear. None of your parts would be retrievable."

Henderson looked at him through Scotch-filled eyes.

"Commander, listen carefully." McLeane leaned

22

into Henderson's face. "With my own eyes I once saw Contardo tear, literally tear, apart a Jap soldier. He pulled the poor bastard open at the mouth and skinned him down to a skeleton."

McLeane poured himself a drink. Henderson was silent. McLeane enjoyed a feeling of self-satisfaction that did not come too often. He turned to Henderson.

"And that, Commander, is a pretty good capsule rundown of the men you mentioned."

Henderson wanted to say something, but a horn interrupted him. A persistent blast sounded throughout the entire ship.

"I have no idea what that's about." Henderson put up his hands defensively. His eyes had suddenly cleared. The horn blast stopped and started again. A crewman stuck his head in the captain's cabin without knocking.

"There's a fight in the mess, sir." If he said anything more neither McLeane nor Henderson heard him as both men beat their way out the door.

The narrow eating quarters looked like a disaster area. Meat, mashed potatoes, peas, and beans, decorated the walls and the deck. Trays and forks lay everywhere. About a dozen sailors sat and stood on one side of the mess guarding their meals. Others could be found crumpled in corners, stretched out cold across tables, or picking themselves up. All four Rangers stood among the debris. None of them spoke. Heinman looked at McLeane sheepishly. O'Connor, still a pale green and unable to speak, rubbed his knuckles. Wilkins shrugged. Contardo

23

stood with his foot on one poor swabbies' head, feeling sorry that the fight had ended so soon. The swabbie moved to get up. Contardo gave him the heel of his boot. His eyes scanned the room, hoping for trouble.

"What does this mean?" Henderson roared, displaying the rage of an angry god, but no one spoke. "Sailor?"

He turned quickly to address an unsuspecting seaman who had not even been involved in the fighting.

"I really don't know, sir." The seaman held a tray that contained eating utensils. "I just came in to eat and—"

"You, sailor?" Henderson turned to another lad.

"Me, sir?" The young man looked up from his tray, surprised.

"Oh, for God's sake!" Henderson wanted to explode.

"Major, sir?" Heinman raised his hand.

"May I, Commander?"

McLeane had not had this much fun in years.

"Heinman, what happened here?"

"Well, these crew members of the good ship Mako referred to us disparagingly as—"

"Shut up, Adolph." Contardo had no patience with words longer than two syllables. "These fucking faggots called us fairies." At the end of the sentence he gave the victim under his boot another shot.

O'Connor did not look well.

"Moreover, sir, the sailor under Contardo's shoe said something about his nose." Heinman stifled a smile.

O'Connor stood weaving on the mess hall deck, holding on to tables. McLeane waited behind Henderson. Henderson surveyed the room.

"Jesus."

Only McLeane heard him.

"I've half a mind to bust every swinging Richard in this room." He eyed each of the men before him. Suddenly, O'Connor broke for the door. Henderson swung around.

"Stop right there, Jarhead!"

O'Connor did and vomited all over two sailors who were struggling to get out of his way.

McLeane tried hard to look serious. He gave O'Connor a quick nod and O'Connor stumbled for the nearest head. The other three Rangers kept straight faces.

On top of everything else, these men could act, McLeane thought, a talent he had not recognized in them before.

Everyone suffered through the long painful silence; then Henderson's shoulders dropped.

"Clean up this place, eat, and get out of here." He sounded defeated.

Back in the captain's quarters McLeane spent many hours making up to the commander. He drank lots of Scotch and listened to many stories of the sea. The word *fairy* had disappeared from their conversation and neither man said anything about the Rangers.

Chapter Three

McLeane said nothing to the Rangers about the ruckus in the mess hall. The "Fearsome Foursome" just slipped off to the quarters the Navy had provided and which, in only a matter of hours, they had learned to call home. They lay in their appointed bunks and waited to fall asleep as the Mako silently slipped by the Caroline Islands toward the Marianas.

Heinman marveled at how little actual noise the sub made. Occasionally the ship vibrated. Other than that he could have been in an air capsule. He wondered what life on board would be like once the Mako and her crew went into action. How did everybody move so quickly in such a confined space? He tucked away his *National Geographic*. He found the stillness of the ship comforting. He thought about Pulusuk and Satawal and all the other parcels of land that lay between the Solomons and the Marianas. Someday he would come back and study them properly, someday after the war.

Contardo entertained no such lofty thoughts. For the past two months he had been troubled by the fate of the Dodgers. Brooklyn's loudest fan only wished he could be back at Ebbetts Field. He knew the Bums needed him. They really stunk. They had no pitching. Besides Stanky nobody on the team looked like a ball player. They should end the season just one place above Philly, he figured, and he had to be at the bottom of the Pacific. Davis, maybe, could get a few over the plate. Maybe they could beat the Giants. All they had to do was beat the Giants.

Next to baseball Contardo thought most of his mother's spaghetti sauce, ambrosia made with tomatoes. At that moment he would have given anything for a heaping bowl of pasta topped with parmigiano. For as far back as he could remember that had been dinner every Tuesday, Thursday, and Sunday. On Sunday all the aunts, uncles, and cousins came to his house, and everyone ate from noon until six in the evening. Could the day be Sunday? Did days of the week exist under water? Being a Ranger in the Pacific one never knew exactly whether the sun came out on a Monday or went down on a Thursday. He liked that. In the absence of any calendar he felt free to name his own days. Vince Contardo, Marine corporal, by the power vested in him, declared that very moment Sunday, and in his mind, he pretended to sit at the oval table in his living room in Flatbush behind a dish piled high with ziti, next to his cousin Amadeo with whom he always fought over the cheese.

Nothing could have been further from O'Connor's mind than food. He had moved from the heaves to the dry heaves, then to just plain, agonizing, wrenching stomach spasms. He clung to the bunk and, half-conscious, prayed to be transported back to Chicago. Out-takes of barroom brawls flashed before him. Chairs flew everywhere. Mirrors broke. Glasses crashed. O'Connor enjoyed blowing up Japs, but for only a moment, he wanted to be back on the South Side pouring beer and shots and kicking asses that got out of line. He tried to smile. Some day he would have his own place.

Wilkins mumbled something unintelligible in his sleep. Contardo looked over at him.

"Hey, hillbilly! Shut the fuck up." Contardo did not like meals, even imaginary ones, interrupted. He rolled over and looked at Wilkins again.

"Why can't you be a gorgeous blonde, huh, instead of a dumb fuck?"

Wilkins never minded such abuse from Contardo. They understood each other. But asleep Wilkins was immune. He dreamed that he was shooting the white rapids where the Ocmulgee River runs down from Macon, beading in on a brown bear scarcely visible through the brush of the Georgia backwoods, running moonshine down from Athens, chased by Feds. He'd never understood how anybody could grow up outside of Georgia. Outside of Georgia all of life seemed dull. He'd never understood the whys and wherefores of places like Brooklyn and Chicago, and he did not want to understand them.

The Mako slowed to a stop and shuddered, but none of the Rangers noticed.

McLeane had checked on the Rangers. Sometimes

29

he felt like a father looking after four bad boys or a kindergarten teacher in charge of problem children. These images did not lift his spirits.

He sat in the mess hall and nursed a cup of coffee. A skeletal kitchen crew puttered over breakfast. Three men on the night watch played pinochle. A lieutenant j.g. sat by himself and read. McLeane looked down at the coffee. No wonder Thompson had a bad stomach. Although the food on board this ship happened to be pretty good, the brown liquid in front of him must have come from the bilge pumps. The pinnochle players slapped their cards on the metal tables. The hand had ended, and the three men counted tricks and laughed. McLeane could smell fresh bread. The Navy did things right. Even under water a baker baked fresh bread.

"Would you like a roll, sir?"

A sailor brought a plate of hot cinnamon buns to McLeane's table.

"Thank you."

He broke one open.

"Do you men always bake like this?"

The sailor smiled.

"It's a little more difficult with depth charges going off around you, but we manage."

McLeane wondered who had cleaned up the mess hall after the Rangers had redecorated it. He hoped none of the sailors had been hurt. He had to laugh. When the Rangers decided to go to work, they went to work. Even Heinman, who under normal circumstances remained the picture of reason, had gotten involved. McLeane doubted there would be any more fighting on this trip, at least not on the Mako.

Besides, Henderson had gone to sleep or had passed out, and he seemed to contribute to the problem. Steam continued to rise off the cinnamon buns. Unable to wait for them to cool, McLeane bit into one. Maybe these sailors couldn't fight, but they definitely knew how to bake cinnamon buns.

Suddenly a picture of Margot flashed across his mind, and he wondered how she might be doing. When he'd left this time she hadn't sulked, pouted, or made his life miserable. For once she had seemed to understand that he did not write his own orders. He missed her. He missed the warmth of her body and her thick red hair. He missed the way she fussed over him, even when it got on his nerves. He missed all of that. He'd even promised not to get involved with another woman on this mission. He'd never understood how those things happened anyway. But he'd promised. He'd even said he loved her. Maybe he did. When he closed his eyes he could see her breasts jiggle under his fatigue shirt. She often wore his fatigue shirt. He wished she could appear with a snap of his fingers.

"Sir, would you care to join us?" McLeane looked up to find one of the pinochle players at his elbow. McLeane recalled his days at Columbia. Then, everyone played bridge. He preferred pinochle players to bridge players, beer to martinis. He played a mean hand of pinochle once.

"Thanks. I think I will." McLeane figured Henderson for a pinochle player and probably not a bad one. He would have liked Henderson more if Henderson had kept his bitterness to himself and not infected his crew with it. He wondered how they held

31

up under fire. He hoped he wouldn't have to find out. He squeezed a sixty meld out of his first hand much to the amazement of the others at the table.

"Tough hand, sir."

"I had some help." McLeane nodded to his partner, who had been no help at all.

On the second hand he ran the table.

"Haven't seen that in a while, sir."

"You need the cards."

"Play much?"

"I haven't played in . . ." McLeane thought about the last time he had played pinochle. He could not remember. He remembered the last time he'd played bridge. Corrigan had lost with his usual lack of grace.

At that exact moment Corrigan sat, ready to lose one more time, but not at bridge. Only a few hours earlier he had flown McKendrick's commandos to the far side of Levuka just behind New Caledonia where Allied intelligence had reported a Jap sub hovering off the coast. Allied intelligence suspected the Japanese might want to establish a communications base there. This bothered the Aussies a great deal. They did not want the Japs that close to their mainland.

McKendrick had volunteered four of Australia's best underwater experts to blow that Jap sub out of the Pacific. He'd also volunteered Corrigan to take them on their mission. After all, what pilot had more experience in sneaking into Japanese territory and in getting out of it? Hadn't McKendrick himself called

Corrigan the best pilot in the RAAF?

Corrigan thought about those very words as he sat under the cover of overgrown dendiki palms while a sudden tropical rain hammered the jungle and he waited for the commandos to return from their job. He wished, just then, that McKendrick had not thought so highly of him. He also wondered momentarily if maybe he had not thought too highly of McKendrick.

He could barely see the near wing of the Catalina in the downpour. The island provided very little natural cover along the shore. He wondered if the palm branches strewn across the nose and over and around the front of the plane as camouflage had fallen off due to the pressure of the rain.

Corrigan held tightly to his Owen, the funny-looking submachine gun shaped like a BB rifle with a top-mounted magazine. The magazine made the barrel easy to clean, but slow to reload in actual combat. The Rangers all laughed and called him Red Ryder. Even the Aussies preferred the American M-1 semiautomatic carbine. Still, Corrigan could make his Owen do anything he wanted. The feel of the metal stock in his hand reassured him. He checked his watch.

In the distance, through the pounding rain, he heard the snap of Jap 97s. McKendrick's men should have done the job already. In fact, they should have been long gone. McLeane's Rangers flashed across his mind. He had less faith in the Australians, but he would never tell McLeane that.

Just then the roof of dendiki palm gave way under the pressure of the rain and a stream of water washed over his head and down his back. He let out an audible "fuck" as the Jap firing increased in the background. With the rain running down his face he readied his Owen. Corrigan had a feeling that at any minute he would be facing the enemy.

Suddenly, a figure crashed through the brush and landed at his feet. In the instant when he was preparing to fire Corrigan recognized one of McKendrick's men. He had been shot up like a Swiss cheese.

"Fucking Japs . . . behind me." He spoke through clenched teeth.

Corrigan did not wait to be briefed. In one move the wiry pilot swung the wounded commando across his back. He heard the Japs coming closer. He fired the Owen with his right hand as they broke for the Catalina, the Aussie's legs, like bloody stumps, flapping on Corrigan's chest.

They fell into the water under the body of the seaplane and Corrigan reloaded. He couldn't see ten yards in front of him.

"Here." Corrigan gave the Aussie his Owen. "Empty this fucking thing into anything that moves."

Lying on his stomach, half covered by the ocean, the Aussie commando, although numbed by pain, fired to cover them.

"And if anything happens to this plane or that weapon," Corrigan called out from the Catalina. "You're staying there."

The Catalina started at once. The Catalina always started at once. Corrigan smiled. He loved the Catalina more than any woman. He went back for the surviving member of McKendrick's squad.

"They're here." Now the wounded commando could speak.

"Thanks for the update."

Corrigan threw his countryman into the Catalina and climbed aboard amidst a hail of Jap bullets.

Suddenly a barrage of fire ripped through the right wing. Corrigan could feel the plane pull. He had to get her into the air. He slammed the throttle full ahead.

"What a fucking mess," Corrigan muttered. The Catalina rose out of the water. Corrigan needed all the skill he had to get her home safely. He would do it. He set his jaw. After a few minutes the Catalina leveled off. Although Corrigan wanted more altitude, he didn't dare risk it.

The whole venture with McKendrick had been a fiasco from the start. Corrigan could not tell just how much damage had been done. Now he had to worry about flak from the ground. He felt like a sitting target. He waited awhile before he spoke. The bad right wing pulled hard. He hated McKendrick.

"Where's McKendrick?"

"Dead." The voice which came from the floor of the plane was strained. The news did not surprise Corrigan.

"What happened back there?" He might have been angrier than he should have been under the circumstances, but Corrigan didn't care. He cared only about the Catalina and getting her back safely.

The Aussie could not be heard over the sound of the engines. He pulled himself closer to the pilot's seat. Corrigan's eyes were peeled straight ahead.

"They were waiting for us."

35

Stupid, Corrigan thought, Of course they were waiting. So what?

"We didn't have a chance."

Corrigan did not want to know the details.

"They hit us with everything."

"How did McKendrick get it?"

"Grenade."

The Catalina hit an air pocket and Corrigan needed all his strength to pull her out of it.

"The rest of them?" Corrigan called out.

After no reply he called out again. "What happened to the rest of them?"

"We never made it to the Jap sub. They were blown right out of the water."

An image of four guys getting strafed and bombed flashed in front of Corrigan. He looked down and saw an island coming up. He couldn't find it on the map. Behind him he could hear the Aussie dying.

"You know, Corrigan, the sub looked so easy out there . . . I tried to detonate it. Nothing went off."

Corrigan could hear him breathing.

"They got me coming back . . . coming back."

Corrigan saw a hand go up. He grabbed it.

"Coming back . . . Shot me down . . . Didn't have a chance . . . No chance . . ."

The Aussie gave Corrigan's hand a hard squeeze, and then he died.

Corrigan didn't even know his name. At that moment he wanted to know the man's name. He knew the names of all the Rangers.

"O'Connor, Wilkins, Heinman, Contardo." He said them out loud. A dying man's hand reached up to him from the floor of the Catalina, and he did not

36

know the name of the man to whom the hand belonged.

Once over the island, antiaircraft fire started. The sky around the plane shook. Corrigan could see clouds of smoke.

"Nice . . . nice." Corrigan held firmly to the controls. "You Nipponese cocksuckers! Nobody gets Corrigan!"

He looked down. "Hey, what's your fucking name?" He kicked the dead hand. "What's your goddamn name?"

With the air blowing up around him and the right wing dipping, Corrigan tried to pick up speed. He still couldn't get over the clouds. Along with everything else there was the rain.

"McLeane, you Yankee son of a bitch. I'm coming home." Corrigan screamed at the top of his lungs, "And you can kiss my Australian ass."

Chapter Four

By the spring of 1944 the Japanese, though exhausted and on the losing end of most battles, still had every intention of winning the war. While the Mako proceeded under water toward the Marianas and Corrigan did everything possible to get the Catalina home safely, two Japanese planned to retaliate against the Americans, and against the Rangers in particular. In Tokyo, Vice-Admiral Jisaburo Ozawa sat in his Emperor's War Department and stared at a map of the Pacific. His eyes remained glued to Saipan. In the jungle just outside General Sasaki's Sixth Army hideaway among the Finisterre Mountains on the Huon Peninsula Major Jinichi Imamura listened to the rain fall on his tent and plotted revenge on McLeane.

Imamura lit up a Chesterfield and remembered well the licking his commandos had taken at the hands of McLeane's Rangers after the battle of Hill

457. Actually, a licking hardly described the encounter. Imamura had selected a dozen of the best troops in the Pacific to retaliate for the Rangers' blowing up the munitions cache hidden below the hill. They'd gone after the Rangers on Vella la Vella. The Rangers had wiped out everyone but Imamura. As the only survivor he had taken the losses hard. Lt. Toshitane Takata, a graduate of the University of Pennsylvania and Imamura's close friend had been among the dead.

Imamura needed to even the score for the death of his countrymen, but he also wanted to avenge his honor. He had lost face in the eyes of General Sasaki, and while his many years at Princeton and his general adaptation to Western ways freed him from a lot of Oriental self-abuse, he needed Sasaki's help to do his job. Without the general's support Imamura would be "retired" to the front lines. Besides, he still had to prove himself.

Major Imamura poured a stiff shot of rye. He preferred Scotch, but during a war one must adapt. He could not even get sake on the black market. Moreover, this occasion, like all occasions since Hill 457, called for whiskey, and he had developed a taste for the stuff. Years ago he'd played snooker and put away shots of rye with beer at a roadhouse on the way to Philadelphia. He could not recall the name of the place, but he remembered a few drunken Friday nights there.

The same source which had procured the rye also had managed to get him a new Nambu. He believed the Japanese would never win the war unless they upgraded their weaponry. The Nambu pistol had to be improved. The old Nambu Type 94 had an externally mounted extension sear and recoiled badly. None of the guns worked properly. He held the Type 11 in his hand and bounced it in his palm. He liked blowback-operated pistols. Imamura sighted, through the entrance to the tent, on a tree. He could barely see through the rain, but he fired. He liked blowback-operated pistols a lot. Now the Japanese had a chance to win the war, and he would help them.

Imamura knew through intelligence sources that the Allies wanted the Marianas. He knew the islands would be hard to take, and he suspected that McLeane would be involved in taking them. He also thought he knew how McLeane and his men would be best put to use. Imamura figured that the Allies had to destroy the Japanese headquarters in the middle of Saipan. He reasoned that only the Rangers could do such close guerrilla fighting successfully. If he, Imamura, were the Allied Commander in the Pacific, he would send McLeane right to the heart of Saipan. Imamura had spent days mulling over these thoughts, and while he had no way of proving his hunches, he would have bet that he was right.

He sat staring out at the rain, reassuring himself that he had to be right when he heard voices. As the voices got louder, Imamura stood. He recognized General Sasaki, surrounded by a cadre of staff officers. The general's voice came at him like a high-pitched whine.

The words, old-world, very formal Japanese, amounted to a condemnation of Imamura's existence on the earth. Put another way, Sasaki wanted to know what gave Imamura a right to live. The general reminded him of the unhappy details concerning Hill 457 and proceeded to call Imamura the Oriental equivalent of a most unspeakable kind of horse's ass. During Imamura's dressing-down, the general's neck got thicker and his eyes bulged. Blood pulsed noticeably through his forehead. Had Major Imamura anything to say for himself? Had he found a way toward redemption since his last dishonor, or had he merely been sitting on his Westernized backside for the last few weeks?

Imamura took all this theater with relative equanimity. After all those years in New Jersey, not too much rattled him. When the general finished, however, Imamura did feel a need to share with him his hunch about Allied future plans as they concerned McLeane.

The general listened, expressionless as Imamura explained all the intricate reasons for why he thought as he did.

The general's eyes widened. He said nothing, walked outside, drew his sword, and with a sudden primordial scream, severed the three lines which, secured to the ground, held up the tent. The tent collapsed around Imamura as the general headed back to his quarters muttering about how much the Emperor had to pay to keep worthless majors in uniform.

The Japanese High Command gathered around Vice Admiral Ozawa as his finger moved along the map on the table through the Solomon Strait, up to the Marianas, to Tokyo, and back again to Saipan.

The august group looked more solemn than usual. None of them needed a lesson in geography to understand Ozawa's point. All of them knew well how the Allies had positioned themselves in the Pacific. A strike on the Japanese mainland seemed only a few islands away.

In the years since Pearl Harbor the Americans, much to the surprise of the Japanese, had managed to produce new fleets of ships and planes. They had developed a technique for island hopping, using amphibious vehicles that remained relatively unknown to the Japanese. The Grumman Hellcat could outfight the Jap Zero in the air. And the Yanks, with help from the Allies, had devised the leapfrog method of bypassing enemy strongholds. They hit the Japs with a barrage of bombs, then landed far behind them on islands that provided landing strips and ports from which to do the same thing all over again somewhere else.

Vice Admiral Ozawa figured the Americans had something like this in mind one more time. They wanted the southern Marianas for air strips and logistics bases. From there they could win the war. Already American naval power dominated the seas. They had 4,700 vessels all over the world, including 613 warships and more than 18,000 planes. That very morning Ozawa had learned that the Americans had nearly 100 fleet and escort carriers in the Pacific alone.

Ozawa spoke slowly and soberly. They, the Japanese, had taken a terrific beating in New Guinea and the Solomons. Knowing that, the Emperor had ordered new planes to be assembled and new pilots trained. Both stood ready. The Japanese had to push now or forget the war altogether.

What did the vice admiral have in mind?

Here, in the area of tactical planning, Ozawa displayed the genius for which he had been justly praised by the Allies as well as the Japanese.

With MacArthur advancing along the New Guinea coast, Ozawa figured Nimitz would probably make his move against Guam, Saipan, and Tinian. A fleet of ships, including subs, had already been spotted heading that way. Ozawa very calmly suggested that the Japanese simply take everything they had and throw it at the Americans. He estimated the Yanks would outnumber them at sea. He knew they had fifteen carriers to the Japanese nine. But, and this became the crux of his argument, the Japanese could take them in the air if they took them by surprise.

No one spoke.

His colleagues, Ozawa added, should not forget the hundred extra planes ready to fly from Guam.

Still no one spoke.

Ozawa looked at his watch. In two days, he reminded everyone, any decision they made would be too late.

The Japanese decided to attack.

Corrigan brought the limping Catalina into Prince of Wales, the northernmost tip of Australia, after a great deal of effort and a whole lot of cussing. A tactical RAF ground crew drove to the improvised dock to meet him. If they seemed a little taken aback by the shape of the awkward-looking flying boat, they stifled their smiles as soon as the tough captain who piloted it came into view.

"He sure looks steamed, sir," a corporal told the lieutenant in charge.

"It's Corrigan," the officer replied as if that explained everything.

"Who, sir?" asked the third member of the crew, a wet-behind-the-ears private.

"Never mind," said the lieutenant. "You'll find out in a second."

They could hear Corrigan yelling at them from forty yards away.

"We'd better wait here," said the lieutenant. "He doesn't look happy, does he?"

The word *cocksuckers* came to them very clearly along with a number of "fuckings" and an emphatic "son-of-a-bitch."

The men got down off the jeep and saluted.

"Captain, sir." The lieutenant accomplished a textbook salute.

"There's a dead man on there," Corrigan said, pointing to the Catalina as he stepped onto the dock and walked by the crew. "Get him off."

"Yes, sir."

Corrigan stopped and turned. "Who's got the radio around here?"

"Sir?"

"The radio, the fucking radio."

The private pointed ahead, but could not speak.

"What's that mean, Private?"

"If you proceed straight ahead, sir," the lieutenant interjected, "you'll see a small cluster of tents. Go to

45

the furthest—"

"Drive me." Corrigan climbed into the jeep.

"But the—"

"You can get him later."

"Yes, sir. But you just can't leave the plane there by the dock without tying her up."

"I can leave that fucking plane anywhere I fucking well want to, Lieutenant. And one of your assholes can tie her up. Now, drive this fucking jeep. After what I've been through in the last twenty-four hours, I would not think twice about blowing you a second asshole."

The lieutenant headed the jeep in the direction from which it had come and pushed it as fast as possible.

"One more thing, sir . . ."

"You *do* have balls, Lieutenant. I'll say that for you."

"Your right wing looks shredded."

"Did you just get out of flight school, or wherever the fuck they send you guys?"

"Well, sir . . ."

"Don't touch that wing. That's my wing."

"Yes, sir."

The jeep slowed, then made a hard right between a row of tents on the edge of the compound.

Corrigan climbed out before the jeep had quite stopped.

"Don't touch that fucking plane," he said without looking back and stormed into the radio shack where a seaman first class sat at a transmitter not much larger than the one on the Catalina.

"Call Bramley for me."

"Sir?"

"Bramley. Call him." Corrigan stared down into a beardless face. The wide eyes that looked up at him had never seen anything quite like Corrigan.

The seaman's voice had suddenly gone dry. "Do you mean Admiral Bramley?"

"How many Bramley's do you know, Seaman?"

The seaman watched the wiry figure pace. Corrigan's khakis were torn; his face was caked with dirt and covered with several days' growth of whiskers. He sat on a folding chair, the only empty chair in the compound. When he got up the seaman did not move, still unsure of what exactly to do.

"I said call him, sailor." Corrigan looked ready to eat someone.

"How? Where is the admiral?"

"Ah, give me that fucking thing." The seaman jumped up before Corrigan threw him out of his seat and moved away while Corrigan fumbled with the radio knobs and muttered. Commander Fanselow and his aide, Lieutenant Granville entered somewhere between a sincere shit and a string of more hearty fucks. When Corrigan, finally, threw the seaman's clipboard across the tent, Commander Fanselow thought he might introduce himself.

"Captain?"

Corrigan got up.

"This thing that you call a radio, Commander, is a piece of shit."

Fanselow, much taller than Corrigan, stood statelier than God and did not bat an eye.

"I can't even get Darwin." Darwin lay a jump across the bay from Prince of Wales, and Admiral

47

Bramley had personal quarters there.

Fanselow held an American Army swagger stick. Corrigan tried not to smile. Suddenly, his anger lost its edge.

"There's nothing in Darwin, anyway, Captain," the commander said evenly and without moving. "Always was a dead town."

The seaman stared straight ahead, happy to be out of the action. The commander's aide stood by the commander's side. Corrigan relaxed.

"I'm trying to get Bramley."

"I know who you're trying to get. He isn't there." Corrigan refused to look nonplused.

"The Admiral is busy with important matters."

"Commander," Corrigan took a deep breath. "I just spent twenty-four hours sitting on some fucking island no one's ever heard of, while four guys died trying to blow up a sub that probably doesn't exist. My plane is fucked and I'm pissed off. I want to reach Admiral Bramley, who sent me on this fucking charade. I would appreciate knowing where he is."

Corrigan tried hard to keep his temper, but Commander Fanselow did not respond at once.

"Commander," Corrigan added.

At that point the commander's aide took Fanselow aside. He spoke only when they were well out of hearing range.

"Commander," said Lieutenant Granville. "We are in the presence of Captain Corrigan."

Nothing registered with the commander.

"He flies the Catalina, sir."

Still the Lieutenant saw no glint of recognition in the commander's eye.

"Well, sir, he flies a lot with the Americans and spends a lot of time behind Jap lines."

Fanselow nodded like someone who did not understand.

"Have you ever heard of McLeane, Commander?" The Lieutenant's voice took on a certain urgency. Still, Fanselow's response was not convincing. The lieutenant broke formal military posture and protocol.

"It's this way, Commander. This is Captain Corrigan. He's Bramley's pride and joy, McLeane's right hand man and the meanest Australian in the whole fucking war. They say he can also fly. Please, Commander, this guy is the worst. Tell him what he wants to know. Give him what he wants. He'd just as soon kill us as them."

"Them?" Fanselow looked around.

All the while Corrigan fidgeted, paced, played with radio knobs, muttered.

"Look, Commander," He walked to where Fanselow stood with Granville. "I—"

"Excuse me, sir." Granville put up both hands. "I have to—"

Corrigan grabbed him by the collar.

"I have to talk to Bramley. I can't reach him. Get him for me."

Granville backed off and tried to rub Corrigan's touch from his uniform.

"I'm gonna kick this cocksucker's nuts right through his fucking eyeballs." Corrigan was not finished. "And the faggot will be out of uniform." He turned away.

Granville put himself between Corrigan and

Fanselow who seemed oblivious to just about everything.

"Sir, you'll be out of uniform." Granville tried his
best. "Your testicles, sir, will be where your eyes
should be, and you won't be able to see. It will be
awful. Imagine being blind and out of uniform."

"Yes," said Fanselow slapping the swagger stick
against his palm. "Out of uniform."

Corrigan threw the seaman's chair across the tent.

"O.K.," Granville blurted out. "Bramley is dealing with the Jap attack."

"What Jap attack?" Corrigan asked.

The commander walked around the tent.

"The attack the Japanese are mounting against the
American fleet that's moving toward the Marianas."
Fanselow spoke.

Corrigan put everything together without help.
He bolted out the entrance. He had not gone a
hundred yards before he sensed the seaman at his
elbow.

"Sir?"

"What the fuck is it?"

"Are you really Corrigan?"

"Kiss my ass." Corrigan headed toward the plane.

"Well, if you're really Corrigan," the seaman
called after him, "the Japs are flying out of Guam
and Bramley's sailing with Halsey and the Yanks."

Corrigan reeled around at the news.

"That, seaman, may be the only useful information I've gotten since I shipped out." He gave the kid
a thumbs-up sign, and the kid smiled.

"Are you really Corrigan?" the kid called after
him. He got the thumbs-up sign one more time. Cor-

rigan broke into a trot. He wanted to find that ground crew. He needed help. The Catalina had to be repaired. Those guys could do it for him. Would the Japs try to fly out of Guam without Corrigan in their way? That Catalina may have been slow and ugly, but Corrigan knew he could take the entire Japanese air force with that one old-fashioned flying box.

"Hey," he found the lieutenant of the ground crew, greeted him, and waved. Then the entire crew followed him. Corrigan had forgotten the fiasco with McKendrick's commandos. He had forgotten McKendrick. Soon he would wage real war.

Chapter Five

On June fifteenth dawn came to the Pacific shortly after four in the morning, at which moment the nose of the Mako cut the surface of the ocean. Except for O'Connor who kept getting more sick instead of less, the rest of McLeane's men headed for the deck.

"Air . . . I need fresh air." Contardo pushed in front of everyone.

"Leave some for the others," Heinman called after him.

"Do you have permission to use your whole nose?"

"Very funny, Wilkins. That's a very funny joke."

Wilkins thought so, and chuckled. They moved quickly up the ladder into the open and found themselves greeted by a fine spray and a tropical, white sky. Contardo spread his arms and took a deep breath.

"Christ," he hollered. "I feel human again."

"Don't push it, Contardo."

"Very funny, Heinman. Heinman made a very funny joke too. Heinman and Wilkins both make funny jokes." Contardo extended a middle finger in their direction.

On all sides, as far as the eye could see, American warships surrounded the submarine.

"Beautiful, huh?" Heinman gestured around him.

"I hope they're on our side." Contardo looked at the carrier close off starboard. "I never seen nothing like that."

They could see the wings of planes stacked along the deck. Figures stood dangerously close to the edge. No one waved as the huge ship churned a stream of white water through the ocean.

Just then O'Connor appeared with McLeane right behind him. Neither one looked as if he had gotten much sleep.

"How do you feel?" Heinman asked.

"Lousy." O'Connor seemed barely able to talk. "Mac thought I should get some air."

McLeane nodded as the wind blew his shirt and pushed against his face. "Bad air down there," he added.

The five men said nothing for a while, impressed by the sight around them, anxious to get their own mission under way.

Major Imamura had a plan, and by the morning of June fifteenth he had decided to approach General Sasaki with it. For the occasion he dressed in full uniform, complete with sword, polished everything that would shine, and practiced a few humble bows. He

54

realized how much his many years at Princeton had estranged him from the ways of his Imperial ancestors. He would defer.

He had expected to wait many hours outside the door until the general deigned to see him. He thought he might have to bow low for several hours. As he made his way through the brush to the command post, he hoped the general would at least be awake. As he got closer, his commando's sixth sense told him something lingered in the air. An amber glow hovered around the corner of the structure Sasaki had fashioned as a conference room.

Two guards stood at port arms on either side of a makeshift lintel from which hung a curtain that separated the inner from the outer circle. He heard voices, but could not understand words.

"Major Imamura would like to see General Sasaki," he told one of the guards.

"The general is busy," came the answer a few moments later. The guard assumed his usual position. Imamura waited.

After a long while, the guard disappeared again into the inner sanctum, only to return immediately. The major had heard the general's voice through the divide.

"You can wait until your ancestors return from the dead." The guard repeated the words of the general.

Imamura waited. Before long, however, his Western background overcame his Eastern ancestry. He straightened himself up and headed for the entrance to the conference room. The guards stopped him, and scowling, he returned to his place in the middle of the outer room. A guard stuck his head into the area where the general and others conferred. At once Lieutenant Colonel Seguchi came out. He looked at Imamura and the two guards.

"Imamura, you are making the general very unhappy." Seguchi spoke the English of a Japanese boy who had lived and gone to school in America. "Serious things are being discussed."

"I, too, have serious things to discuss with the general."

They spoke English so the guards would not understand. Imamura liked the way Seguchi combined Japanese politeness and patience with an American sense of urgency about getting the job done.

"Can you share this serious business with me?" If they had not been close friends, they had not been antagonists either. The two of them moved farther away from the guards.

"I want McLeane. I believe he will go to Saipan. I must get him."

Imamura tried to justify his hunch to Seguchi, tried to explain how he thought the Rangers would be sent to clear away the guerrillas so that the regular troops could move through the island more easily. Seguchi listened with Japanese politeness and patience.

"At this moment our fliers are attacking the American fleet moving up the Marianas," he said. "The general has much on his mind. I think there is merit in what you say, however, and I will talk to him as soon as possible." Lieutenant Colonel Seguchi bowed, turned, and left.

Major Imamura stood silently, waiting for Lieutenant Colonel Seguchi to return.

When the colonel came back, at last, he asked, "What do you need?"

"Four men," said Imamura without moving. "One for each of them."

"You must need more than that."

"The general knows what I need. Four men . . . and a pilot to fly us out, someone very good. I need someone who knows how to fly at night, fly silently and—"

"Thank you, Major. You will have what you need." The colonel went back inside.

A terrible screaming came from the general's conference room. Imamura heard only Sasaki's voice. Then Seguchi appeared and handed Imamura a folder.

"Take any four men you want," he said, "and leave as soon as possible."

The folder contained information on all the men stationed with the general at his hideaway.

"I shall need a pilot," said Imamura.

"I will fly you."

Imamura said nothing. The colonel smiled. "I can fly, Major," he said. "Believe me."

Imamura turned to leave.

Seguchi called after him.

"If we do not succeed, Major, the general says we must fall on our swords."

Imamura gave him the thumbs-up sign. They both laughed.

At first the ground crew didn't do anything right,

according to Corrigan. Then it didn't do enough. Finally, it didn't do anything at all. No one knew how to repair the Catalina properly.

"Not like that, you assholes," Corrigan yelled. "Gently. She's a woman, not a fucking elephant. You're trying to fix the wing, not tear it off."

When the crew finally learned how Corrigan wanted his special baby treated, they could not move fast enough.

"Are you guys sleeping? I don't have that kind of time. Move your asses." Corrigan wanted to get at those Japs so badly that every minute on the ground seemed like a day.

"This guy's a loony," one crew member said to the lieutenant just loudly enough for Corrigan to hear.

"That may be, but you keep working," Corrigan called over, "or I'll have you busted down to your fucking socks."

The men worked—cutting, bolting, tying, welding—until they could barely lift their arms, and Corrigan worked alongside, over, under, around, and ahead of them. When they could no longer see, he found a search light and, in violation of every security regulation of any armed force, threw whole shafts of light on the Catalina all night long.

"Shit, we're sitting ducks," muttered one crew member.

"The Japs will bomb us into next week," said another.

Meanwhile, Corrigan held and pulled and pushed and screamed out orders to men standing less than two feet from him.

When no one had the strength to work anymore,

58

when day had come again and gone, Corrigan kept going.

"Candyasses," he called out periodically to the men lying about exhausted. "The Australian navy has enlisted girls . . . sissies . . . a whole fucking navy of sissies."

The men, too tired to care about anything but sleep, just lay there.

"He's the biggest fucking nut I've ever seen," said the lieutenant as the sun came up and Corrigan still stood by the wing of the Catalina, bare chested and dirty.

"Well, girls, we're done." Corrigan had not stopped calling them names for the better part of a day and a half. "Now where can I fuel up?"

The lieutenant just pointed. Corrigan fired up the Catalina and taxied around the bay. He had a good 1,200 nautical miles to go.

On the morning of June fifteenth Corrigan headed out for the Marianas to meet the Japanese Air Force, leaving a Prince of Wales that would never be the same without him. As the Catalina lifted off, the right wing pulled only slightly. Corrigan threw the throttle to full and flew straight ahead over open ocean.

He looked down onto a pale blue floor. He had not slept. He didn't need sleep. He smiled, then broke out into a robust chorus of "Waltzing Matilda." He had not eaten. He did not need food. Vice Admiral Ozawa would soon learn what Commander Fanselow, Lieutenant Granville, and the ground crew at Prince of Wales already knew: there is a Corrigan.

Chapter Six

"*Princeton.* That's the USS *Princeton.*" Contardo read the name of the carrier sailing parallel to the Mako. "Some fucking boat."

"Ship," a member of the sub crew said. "In the Navy we call them ships."

Contardo knew what they called them. He just liked to irritate the swabbies. This constant need to aggravate other human beings constituted most of his charm, as Heinman would often remind him.

"Yeh, some fucking big boat," Contardo said, a little louder.

"You're quite a good chap, Contardo," Heinman said. "You really have a way with people."

Contardo smiled from ear to ear. The sailors kept their mouths shut.

McLeane had gone below to find out from Henderson why the Mako had surfaced in daylight. Given the sensitivity of their mission and the fleet's proximity to the Marianas, McLeane did not think it wise to have done so. McLeane had come to believe that Henderson did not have a great tactical mind. Wilkins went back to get some sleep.

O'Connor stood away from the rest of the Rangers, by himself against the rail, and watched the Pacific slip behind him. His only other experience with water had been as a chaser for whiskey. That thought didn't comfort him. His stomach continued to pull down around his knees, but he felt somewhat better in the fresh dawn air than he had in the cramped compartment below.

His eyes scanned the horizon. In the distance, coming toward them, he could make out three specks in the sky.

"Hey," he called out, unable to say anything more, pointing overhead.

Everyone moved quickly to where he stood.

"How do we get down from here?" Heinman wanted to know.

"Zeros," muttered one of the sub crew.

"How do we get down from here *fast*?" Contardo did not mind facing enemy aircraft on land too much, but on the ocean he did not like them at all.

O'Connor vomited over the rail.

One of the sailors yelled into an intercom. Then a squadron of Hellcats took off from the deck of the *Princeton*. Everyone on the bridge of the Mako watched as the Americans tried to engage the Japanese. The Japanese, however, seemed to have some other mission.

"Look at those fuckers go," said Contardo as the enemy planes outmaneuvered the Hellcats. He could have been watching an air show at some state fair.

"Something doesn't look right to me," Heinman volunteered. O'Connor just shook his head in agreement.

"They're not Zeros. They're Tony's—kamikazes," a sailor snapped. "They're going after the *Princeton*."

He lit a Camel and, without taking his eyes off the battle in the sky overhead, passed it to Contardo who took a drag and passed it back. The Hellcats handled one Tony, but the other two flew under the attack and headed straight for the carrier. A couple of U.S. planes followed.

"The *Princeton* can't use her guns," said the sailor. "She don't have many and they might hit their own planes."

"You mean they just got to watch this?" Contardo had anger in his voice.

"Pretty much."

Sirens sounded aboard the *Princeton*.

"I can't get the Captain on the horn," said the sailor.

"O.K., everyone below." As the officer of rank, Heinman put himself in charge. Neither of the Rangers moved. Two sailors disappeared through a hatch on the deck. The other stayed on the horn.

"We've got to get this ship under, Lieutenant," he told Heinman. "It's bad up here."

"Contardo! O'Connor! Get below!"

"Fuck you." Hell would freeze before Contardo ever took an order from Heinman. O'Connor just shook his head in refusal. Both American planes were out of sight, behind the hull of the great aircraft carrier. The Hellcats circled back. Then came the noise. Billows of fire and smoke shot from the aft deck of the *Princeton*. The Rangers could not see much, but they imagined a lot.

The sailor looked up.

"I have Major McLeane on the horn. He wants everybody below on the double."

The Mako's dive bell sounded, a loud repeated clang.

"That means we're going under."

Then, out of the sky, from the opposite direction and flying low came a Zero.

"He's coming for us."

Everyone hit the deck. The Zero strafed the sub and passed overhead. The men on deck scurried for the hatch. O'Connor glanced overhead to see three Hellcats engage the lone enemy plane. The last man scampered below just in time to close the lid before water spilled onto the ship.

Once they were below, the men collected themselves.

"Where's the swabbie?" Contardo noticed that the sailor was missing.

Some of the crew had gathered around the Rangers.

"The Jap got him." Heinman had seen the whole thing. "A shot went right through his head. He didn't know what hit him."

"Well, I hope we don't run into more trouble," said one of the crew, "because that was the best torpedo mate in the Navy."

No one spoke for a long while. Then the Rangers

went back to their compartment and woke up Wilkins.

"Where's Mac?" Contardo asked.

"I don't know." Wilkins lay in his bunk, still half asleep.

"He's in with the captain," said a voice behind them. "I'm Ensign Pete Meskin."

A small, thin, very young man smiled and reached out his hand. All the Rangers took it and introduced themselves.

"Yep, our captain is a little under the weather, and your major is helping him out, you might say."

In the Captain's quarters McLeane tried sobering up a very indisposed Lieutenant Commander Henderson. McLeane had poured pots of black coffee laced with salt into the skipper, forcing him to throw up at least a quart of gin. Finally, the chief executive officer of the Mako sat not quite wide-awake, shaky, and a little sick, sipping hot water with lemon.

"Look, McLeane . . ." Henderson had difficulty expressing what was on his mind. "I, uh, don't usually make . . . I . . ."

"Forget it," McLeane wanted no apologies from life or people. A man did or didn't do a job, depending on a lot of things, but he always kept his mouth shut.

Henderson's face was ashen, and his eyes looked like a couple of taillights. He had trouble holding the cup of hot water and just sat while McLeane studied the navigation chart.

"Can you read one of those things?"

"Yes." Such questions always amused McLeane. The Navy forgot that, theoretically at least, the Marines lived half their lives on water.

"It's 0543."

"Yes, I know. According to the last reading we're running late. McLeane looked around to see Henderson bent over.

"I don't feel too well, Major."

Some people drink to be sociable, some to forget, and some to kill themselves, McLeane thought to himself. Henderson fell into the last category.

"Drink is a form of suicide in which one has a chance to return from the dead," McLeane said. He heard the skipper chuckle.

"Not bad."

A loud bang interrupted their poetic contemplation, not too soon for McLeane. He opened the door to find a young sailor he recognized as the radioman standing before him at attention.

"Sir, may I speak with the skipper?"

The major can hear anything you want to tell me." Henderson called out from his seat at the table. His voice managed to show authority despite the shakes his whole body continued to suffer.

"This just came in, sir." The sailor handed McLeane a piece of paper.

"Read it, Talbot, for Christ's sake. Nobody understands that crap you write."

"We're being attacked," McLeane said glancing at the message. "This whole fleet, Commander, of which this submarine is a part, can expect to be greeted by about three hundred Jap aircraft."

"When are they coming?"

"Any minute now," said McLeane.

"Is that right, Talbot?"

"That's right, sir."

"That's what that kamikazes were for," McLeane said.

"They got Weisner," Talbot added.

"The torpedo mate?"

"Yes, sir."

Henderson put his head in his hands.

"Very often the Japs will send kamikazes in to take out a carrier before a heavy air attack." McLeane knew about kamikazes. He had seen more of them do their work than he wanted to remember.

Talbot waited to be dismissed, then just disappeared when Henderson didn't move.

McLeane glanced around the cabin: a bunk, neatly made, a sink with a mirror above it, the table where Henderson sat and three empty chairs, and the table where McLeane stood, on it a detailed map of the Pacific stretched across an oversize board illuminated by a single tensor light. Two wall lockers were crowded in next to the entrance.

He found himself surrounded by cold steel and gray walls. Bolts showed through and pipes ran across the ceiling barely clearing his head. What a depressing place to spend one's days, he thought.

"McLeane?" Henderson still sat, looking down. "Do you know that this crew has been . . ." His voice trailed off. "Forget it," he said.

"We're in for trouble, Major." Henderson thought he would try again on a more upbeat note. He moved to get up, but fell back into his chair. "Whenever you have air attacks on the water, you have carriers, and whenever you have carriers, you—"

"Have destroyers," McLeane picked up the conversation without dropping a syllable. "And where you have destroyers, submarines have trouble . . . lots of trouble."

McLeane wanted a cup of coffee.

"I see you know." Henderson clutched his stomach.

"Do you have another problem, Henderson?" McLeane had had some experience with hangovers. The victim didn't usually double over in pain. He might lie prone, even for a couple of days. His head might hurt and his world might swim, but after a little while, his stomach was never more than slightly upset.

"Ulcers." Henderson grunted out the answer.

"Do you have medication?"

Henderson shook his head from side to side.

General Thompson had a nervous stomach. McLeane had an aunt with colitis. He could only imagine an ulcer, and he imagined a hot point in the gut where someone might have stuck a glowing, red poker. People with ulcers drink milk, he remembered.

"Want some milk?"

"Yeah. And tell the first officer I want him to go to periscope depth and find out what the hell's going on up there."

Ensign Meskin procured some contraband Australian hootch which he shared with the Rangers. O'Connor, usually a great drinker, at that moment could not bear to even smell the stuff, and with the help of gestures and an occasional dry heave, he managed to get across to everyone that they should go away. So the four men left the Rangers' cramped compartment, not, however, without a few kind words from Contardo.

"No guts, O'Connor. That's your problem. You're just a dumb, chicken-shit, Irish fuck."

O'Connor, too sick to even pay attention, just held on to his bunk.

"You really know how to cheer up people, Contardo. And you have such a kind way with words," said Heinman on their way out the door.

"Why, thank you, Adolph. That means a lot to me coming from you." Contardo wore a big grin. "You always got to get a guy when he's down, especially O'Connor."

"Don't get the wrong idea," Heinman said to Meskin. "It's one of the great love-hate relationships. They've saved each other's lives so many times neither keeps track anymore."

The mess hall had filled up, but the ensign found a quiet corner anyway, and they all sat down.

"These men have been through a lot," Meskin said. "They've been under water so much I'm surprised their skin isn't wrinkled."

"That bad was it?" Heinman decided not to tell him what the Rangers had been up to for the last two years.

"And the Old Man's had it. He's ready to crack. Maybe he's cracked already. We've been losing crew the way some people lose umbrellas. I don't know half these guys."

"How do you lose them?" Contardo knew nothing about submarines.

"A few get it like Weisner, but most of them can't take the life and have to be put ashore."

Contardo did not understand anyone being unable to put up with anything, except maybe the New York Yankees. Ensign Meskin lost his winning smile.

"Have you ever been in a sub under attack? Have you ever been stuck at the bottom of the ocean, unable to make a sound while a couple of destroyers drop depth charges on you?"

Contardo could not say that he had ever been there.

"Do you know what it's like when a depth charge hits close to the ship? You feel the vibrations in the middle of your stomach. The whole ship rolls, and you can't do a thing about it. You can't even whisper 'shit' because they'll hear and get you next time for sure."

Contardo would always find something to do about anything, and he could not imagine being unable to say shit.

"Shit is half of Contardo's vocabulary." Heinman wanted to change the conversation to something less serious. "What's the other word you know?"

"Fuck you."

"That's it. That's the one."

Contardo reached over to where Wilkins sat quietly and twisted his nose. Wilkins quickly brought a hand to his face.

"What's that for?"

"I just want to know if you're alive, Wilkins. You're too quiet. Do something so I know you're out there. You make me nervous not saying nothing."

"Not everyone is as informed as you on so many topics. Now, leave the man alone." Heinman shook his head and smiled. Meskin could not quite believe Contardo.

"And this fucking place stinks." Contardo would not let up.

"Hope that's as bad as it gets."

Chapter Seven

Actually, the Japs had already moved in. Heinman, stuck below the Pacific, could not possibly know that. Even as he spoke Ozawa's rebuilt air force, new Zeros manned by fresh pilots, filled the sky above the Mako, attacked the fleet speeding toward the Marianas, and sought out U.S. Hellcats and Corsairs. They did not have to seek far. Seconds after the first Japanese aircraft had borne down on an American battleship, nine U.S. carriers had put planes in the air.

At first, the Zeros outranged the American planes, and the young Japanese flying them kept the Americans on the defensive with their aggressive acrobatics. For the early hours of the engagement the Yanks just tried not to get shot down. But then the tables turned, and American experience and numbers began to make themselves felt. With so many carriers close by, the Americans did not have to go far to refuel, while the Japanese planes had to go back and forth to Guam. So, in time, the Hellcats and Corsairs had taken the offensive and were blowing the Zeros out of the sky.

For the Rangers, however, the Japanese presence at sea presented a far greater and more immediate threat than the Japanese presence in the air. In addition to throwing the entire Japanese air force at the Americans, Ozawa, in a final effort to keep the Americans from overrunning the Pacific, also hit them with what was left of the Imperial Navy. His fleet included nine carriers. On balance, the Americans overwhelmed the Japs at sea. But they posed an enormous problem for the Mako. A Japanese sub located the Mako. Soon, a couple of enemy destroyers also knew her exact location. Fortunately, the first Jap torpedo went wide, missing the Mako but giving the American crew the warning they needed.

The first mate stuck his head in the open door of the captain's quarters.

"Sir, we're under attack. Sub off starboard."

Henderson said nothing and did not move.

"Sir . . ."

"Drop her straight down. Three hundred feet." Suddenly McLeane took over. "And fast."

The mate looked at Henderson, then back at McLeane. McLeane just gave his head a quick and reassuring nod and the mate disappeared.

"Half these guys have never seen a battle, and the other half haven't seen anything else for two years." McLeane knew which half Henderson belonged in, but he had no desire to be hard on the guy. He certainly didn't want to give orders. But someone had to do something, and he found himself the officer of rank on board.

In the mess, Ensign Meskin and the Rangers heard the alarm sound before they felt the Mako dive. Meskin shot a worried glance at the other three.

"I don't know what this means," he said, "but I've got to get to my battle station."

For the first time in action, Heinman thought, none of the Rangers had a battle station to get to. In fact, none of them had anything to do. Even Wilkins felt a little awkward as the mess hall emptied out.

"Let's see O'Connor," suggested Contardo, for want of anything else to do. They arrived at their compartment to find O'Connor sound asleep.

"Leave him alone," Heinman said before Contardo had a chance to do anything like jump on the Irishman's head or shout abuse at him. One of O'Connor's arms hung over the side of the bunk.

"Quick," Contardo said to Wilkins. "Get a bucket of warm water."

"What?" Wilkins thought he might not have heard correctly.

"A bucket of warm water . . . Get me a bucket of warm water."

"What for?"

"Just do it."

"Nope."

"Look," Contardo's face broke into an impish grin. "We stick his hand in a bucket of warm water and watch him piss himself." Contardo started to laugh. Wilkins showed no sign of having understood.

"It's like this," Contardo continued. "Get a guy who's asleep. Stick his hand in warm water, and he pisses himself . . . and we watch him."

"Get out of here." Heinman grabbed Contardo by the back of the collar. Contardo, laughing too hard to resist, went easily.

"Contardo, I don't believe you sometimes," Heinman said when they were in the narrow corridor which ran through the center of the ship. "Besides, it doesn't work."

"It did in boot camp." Contardo could hardly talk he was so busy laughing and slapping his palms against the gray metal wall that lined the Mako. "The guy woke up swimming in fucking piss."

"It doesn't work." Gently, Heinman pushed Contardo ahead of him. With the sub on alert and deep in enemy territory, Contardo *had* to play practical jokes. Heinman chuckled and shook his head.

The alert had stopped and the crew members no longer milled around. In the stillness Heinman envisioned three pranksters gamboling down a forbidden alley as he and the two other Rangers made their way straight ahead in the dim light. In corners and alcoves they found crewmen standing quietly by their equipment. In the main body of the ship the rest of the crew sat, silent and motionless. Technicians manned sonar and radio sets. The men's breathing sounded in the thick, stale air. Meskin stood tensely by the periscope.

"Where's Mac?" Contardo did not think anyone

could whisper more softly. Meskin just shook his head. Heinman put a finger to his lips.

The explosion came just when everyone, though ready, least expected it. The lights flickered, then went out. Red emergency lights went on. The whole ship shook. Contardo grabbed his boot for the knife he always carried. Wilkins reached for an automatic. Meskin noticed and smiled. The second one hit closer.

Depth charges, Contardo thought. He knew that much. He also knew the third time could be the last. Personally, he would not mind fighting the whole Jap navy single-handed, but on land.

"Fuck this shit," he said suddenly and, knife still in hand, stumbled out into the corridor.

"What's wrong with you?" Heinman followed close on his heels. "Are you mad? Where do you think you're going?"

The corridor seemed even darker than the compartment.

"It stinks in there."

"Since when did odors bother you?"

"This place is for loonies. Let's go back and watch O'Connor piss himself. Believe me it works. Or let's go find Mac."

"Let's go find the major," Wilkins piped up. He could not comprehend the fascination in watching other guys piss—especially O'Connor. He had seen O'Connor piss lots of times. The experience did nothing for him.

Before Heinman had a chance to decide, Contardo had pushed off into the dark down the central passageway that ran from fore to aft in every sub. At one point, Heinman and Wilkins heard a resounding thud.

"What happened?" Heinman whispered.

"I bumped my fucking head," Contardo responded.

"At least nothing got hurt."

Suddenly, Contardo found no deck under him. He had made a quick move forward and then felt himself dropping. He didn't fall far but the shock set his blood racing.

"Hey." He wanted to warn the others, but he was too late. They came tumbling down on top of him.

"Shit, they're diving."

Before any of the Rangers had a chance to speak they noticed voices. They had fallen near the engine room, and could hear the engineers talking.

"We can't take it lower.... Fucking thing'll break in half."

" . . . engines'll give us away."

"Yeah, can't make no sounds."

"The bottle's finally got to the Old Man."

The sub shuddered when the electric engines sped up. The noise level rose as the ship moved off, then slowly down.

"I don't like this shit, man." Contardo almost sounded as though he was afraid. "Let's get out of here."

"Where you want to go?" Wilkins did not have Contardo's imagination.

"Who gives a fuck as long as it's away from here." With that, having no idea what lay above, he hoisted himself up. The others followed.

*   *   *

78

"Take her down."

"More, sir?" The first mate had doubts,

"Down."

Both men spoke so softly they could hardly hear each other. The first mate had spent the last two years on board the Mako and knew everything about submarines. McLeane knew nothing about submarines, but a great deal about battle. In battle, according to McLeane, the good guys win. To do that, they have to get away from the bad guys when the bad guys think they have the good guys trapped. Then the good guys have to get the bad guys when the bad guys least expect it. These simple rules applied in water as well as on land. In their situation, the bad guys thought they had the good guys trapped. As a good guy, McLeane felt responsible for getting away, however he could manage to do so.

"Sir?" The first mate raised his voice as the sub crept lower. "Sir, I'm afraid the hull won't take the pressure."

For all McLeane knew the mate was right, though he had never heard of a sub splitting apart from the weight of water. To get away from two destroyers, however, he knew he had to go deeper. The destroyers would find it harder to judge depth. A lesser depth made the Mako more vulnerable. Their motion could be more easily detected. By going lower, the Mako was forcing the enemy sub to do the same. The Japs would have to reach the same level as the Mako to make their torpedoes effective. McLeane derived some amusement from picturing the Japs worrying over whether or not their own sub would crack under so much pressure.

"Lower," McLeane said with the hint of a smile.

The first mate obeyed the order. The strains on the sub's joints sounded throughout the entire ship. McLeane lit a Chesterfield. The Mako dropped more.

"All stop."

The first mate cut the engines. The sub slowed to a halt. Everyone waited.

The explosion that followed rocked McLeane's teeth, but he neither moved nor changed the expression on his face. The first mate got thrown against the wall. He shook himself as he slowly rose. No one spoke for a while.

"A charge has never come that close without being a hit." The mate tried to clear his head. Had they been any higher, the Mako would have been blown to bits. He looked at McLeane with newfound admiration.

"Ahead one quarter. Right full rudder. Silent running."

"We could get killed, Major."

"What else is new?"

McLeane remembered a time at the outset of the war, before General Thompson had chosen him for Ranger duty, when the impact from Jap artillery knocked a young lieutenant off the jeep in which they were both riding. In a four-foot fall to the ground the lieutenant broke his neck.

A depth charge went off to port.

"You called that one right, sir," the first mate said rubbing his shoulder.

"What's the location of the enemy sub?"

The mate stuck his head into the room where most of the crew sat in near darkness.

"Get Swanson in here."

McLeane recognized the bald and burly Swanson as the sonar operator.

"Sir."

"Where's the enemy sub?"

"Well, sir, as near as I can tell, and it's only a guess, about five hundred yards off starboard, and back up near the surface. I guess she couldn't take the depth as well as we could."

"That puts her under the other destroyer."

"Just about, sir."

"We're under one destroyer, and she's under the other."

"Let me know exactly how far down she is, Swanson."

"I read fifty feet, sir."

"Thanks."

"Do this." McLeane turned to the mate. "Plot a course toward that sub and move out slowly."

"We going after her, sir?"

"That's the general idea." McLeane answered. Just how he had not yet figured out. A voice interrupted his thoughts.

"Schuyler's hurt, sir."

McLeane looked at the first mate.

"You stay there. I'll look at him."

He made his way through the still, tense bodies, into the dark corridor forward of the conning tower to an alcove where a form sat propped against a bulkhead.

"We both got pretty badly shaken up in that last blast, Sir." McLeane looked at a tall, willowy kid no more than eighteen. He figured the youth was a new member of the crew. McLeane knelt down by his partner, who could not have been much older. Even in the near dark he could tell what had happened. McLeane got up without a word.

"Is he O.K., sir?" The boy sounded frightened.

McLeane looked at him.

"He's dead."

"Are you sure?" McLeane could tell the kid wanted to cry.

"Very." McLeane put his hand on the boy's shoulder.

McLeane knew about broken necks, but said nothing and walked away. Behind him he could hear the kid whimper. He reentered the room of frozen, stinking bodies. As he ducked through the portal to where the first mate stood at the controls, he noticed, in the red light, three familiar figures.

"Hey, you know what's funny?"

"Shut up." He could not mistake Contardo.

"Why do I have to shut up? I never say—"

"Shut up." When Contardo got hold of a couple of good words, he never let go.

"Hello, sir."

"Hi, Heinman." McLeane chuckled. The Marx Brothers flashed in front of him.

"Sir?"

"Forget it, Heinman." Then the idea hit him. As he looked at the Rangers in front of him, he figured out how to sink the Jap sub.

Chapter Eight

The *Mako* crept silently toward the Japanese submarine. McLeane was surrounded by Rangers, the first mate, and Ensign Meskin.

"Here's what's going to happen. When Swanson gets us a little closer, we're going to bring this baby up to her level. Load all bow tubes and set the torpedoes for fifty feet."

"A sub-to-sub hit without a visual fix is a million to one," the mate said.

"It's been done before. In the Solomons, I think."

Meskin said, "That was in a narrow strait, Major. We're in open seas."

"I don't understand something," Contardo said.

"Tell me something I don't know," McLeane snapped.

"Why do we have to go after the sub?" Contardo asked.

McLeane glanced at the two sailors. "Correct me if

I'm wrong. We could probably hide from the destroyers and sooner or later one of our battleships or a few planes would take them out. They don't worry me too much.

"The sub is another matter. We can't run hard without our engines telling her where we are, and with those two Jap tin cans upstairs we can't rely on our surface ships to take her out. Even if we could hide from her, we're supposed to be on schedule. If we have to spend three days fucking around and hoping not to get torpedoed, we might as well go home."

"I don't know about this, Major," Heinman said.

"A number of things could happen. We could get the enemy sub. If we do, so much the better. If we don't, those Jap destroyers could pick up the high-speed screws of our torpedoes that miss the Jap sub and they might think that their own ship is firing on them. We could get those Nip destroyer hotshots to mistake their own sub for us. Besides, you don't win games if you don't take chances."

Heinman thought for a while, then said, "I vote against the plan."

"Since when did this unit become a democracy?" McLeane asked. "I told you what we were doing and why. I did not ask for your opinion, let alone your vote."

"Sorry, sir."

"And stop calling me 'sir' all the time. It makes me feel like a damned admiral. Now, let's get going with this . . . little adventure."

McLeane crossed the room to ponder the pings coming from the sonar set.

"That guy's got some pair of balls," said the first mate.

"The biggest in the Pacific," Contardo agreed.

McLeane looked over Swanson's shoulder as the sonar mate twiddled the knob that directed the tiny pulses of sound. McLeane's confidence had put some guts back into the leaderless sub crew.

"Starboard two," Swanson said.

The helmsman echoed the command. "Starboard two."

"Five degrees up angle."

"Five degrees up."

The pings were louder. Swanson turned to look at McLeane. "We're three hundred and fifty yards from the target and closing."

"What's the safety factor in yards for us?"

"Two-fifty at the most, after the depth pressure we've just taken."

"We'll fire at three hundred yards," McLeane said. "Will we be at fifty feet then?"

"Aye, sir," another voice said. "Reaching seventy now. We're at seventy feet, Major."

"Keep bringing her up, nice and slow."

Swanson said, "Helm to neutral. Ahead dead slow."

"Sixty feet."

"Can you hear anything else?" McLeane asked. "Background noise. Fish farting. Anything?"

"I'm getting heavy screws, Major. All sides, and converging."

"The Jap tin cans?"

"No, sir. Bigger and heavier. Battlewagons or

85

heavy cruisers."

"Ours," McLeane said confidently.

Swanson said: "Wait a second. Lighter screws, turning rapidly. Major, I think those Jap destroyers are getting the hell out of here!"

The sonar man said that they were at fifty feet, the same as the Japanese submarine.

"Level off," the first mate said. "Distance to target?"

Swanson counted off the yards. "Three-twenty . . . three-ten . . . Major, I'm getting the sound of slow speed screws. The sub's taking off too."

"Holding at fifty feet."

"Three hundred yards," Swanson said.

"Fire!" McLeane snapped.

"Tube one—fire," the first mate said.

"Tube one fired."

"Tube two—fire!"

"Tube two fired."

When all four torpedos were launched, McLeane growled, "Let's us get the hell out of here too."

"Port twenty," the first mate said, his confidence reestablished. "All ahead flank."

"Time to target?" Meskin asked.

Swanson counted down from twenty seconds. When he got to one second, the *Mako* shook as if grabbed by Jules Verne's giant squid.

Swanson tossed off the headphones. "Got her!" he yelled, and his cry was echoed up and down the length of the *Mako*.

There was a second explosion. Swanson put his headphones back on. "She's breaking up."

"What about the heavy screws?" McLeane asked.

"Three thousand yards and converging. The Jap destroyers are moving out of sonar range."

McLeane smiled. "Well, gentlemen, I think we'd better surface and show our colors before our battlewagons mistake us for someone we're not."

"Amen to that," the first mate said. "Blow tanks one and two. Ten degrees up angle. Emergency surface."

His orders were repeated. McLeane and the Rangers hung on while the *Mako* shot to the surface.

"Those screws sound like cruisers to me," Swanson said. "Two cruisers closing, one carrier farther away."

"They're protecting the carrier," the first mate said. "Radio!"

"Aye!"

"Prepare to broadcast our I.D. upon surfacing."

"Yes, sir."

"There's not much sense in going through all this just to get blown out of the water by our own guys, is there?"

"Not much, no," McLeane said.

The *Mako* broke the surface in the middle of the worst battle McLeane had ever seen. As he followed the first mate up onto the bridge, water soaking the two of them, the skies all around were lit with smoke, tracers, planes, and debris. The clattering of the anti-aircraft batteries and the buzz of aerial combat drowned out the emergency surface horn of the *Mako*.

"Jesus H. Christ," the first mate said.

"It looks like we're kickin' some ass," McLeane agreed.

The two cruisers bearing down on the *Mako* recognized the submersible as one of their own and turned away in pursuit of the enemy destroyers. McLeane flinched as their eight-inch forward turrets spat hundred-pound shells in the direction of the enemy ships.

The first mate scanned the horizon, took a few bearings, then ordered the navigational officer to plot a new course for Saipan.

Another voice came from another direction. "Nice work, Major," Henderson said.

The captain was unsteady, but walked to McLeane and shook his hand. "I don't know if anyone could have done better."

"Are you okay now?"

"I'm not about to run in the Olympics, but I'm holding my own."

He put his arm around McLeane's shoulders. "I'm sorry I fucked up so badly. I guess that three years of this has gotten to me. Of course, I'll put myself on hack as soon as we reach base."

McLeane bristled. "Bullshit you will. We all fuck up now and then, Captain. You happened to fuck up at the wrong time. I won't lie and tell you it hasn't happened to me. You came down with the flu. That's it, and I don't want to hear any more about it."

"I lost it, McLeane. I endangered many lives."

"No lives were lost. No damage was done, and that's the bottom line. If I might suggest something? . . ."

"Name it?"

"Drink under palm trees, not out on the Pacific. That way when you fall down, all you hurt is your pride."

By noon of June fifteenth Vice Admiral Ozawa had a pretty good idea that his new planes and his fresh, young pilots could not hold the skies against slower American planes flown by older, more experienced men. In fact, he had to admit that on that day the heavens over the Marianas might well have been the arena for the most mismatched foes in modern warfare.

Ozawa could not comprehend the speed with which the Americans responded to the Japanese challenge, and he could not begin to imagine how they counterattacked so effectively in such a short time. Actually, American radar gave the Yanks advance warnings so they had more than enough time to do just about anything they had to do. When the Japanese approached the Pacific Fleet, the Americans already had their planes warmed up and waiting, and U.S. bombers were on the way to destroy the Guam airfields which provided sanctuary for over one hundred enemy planes.

G.I.s came to call that air battle "the Day of the Great Marianas Turkey Shoot." While that went on above, the Pacific Fleet overwhelmed the Imperial Navy. The Japs lost three carriers and two oilers to American subs right off the bat, from then on the battle went badly for the emperor's ships. The Americans not only overpowered the Japanese with material, they outfought them. Heroism carried the day. When American planes returned, in the darkness and out of gas, the skipper of the flagship *Lexington* ordered all ships to turn on their lights so the planes could see. This defied standard operating procedure. Given the presence of submarines, such a bold action made every United States ship vulnerable to attack. That same action, however, also allowed pilots to land or to ditch their planes in the ocean near the ships. Rescue crews managed to save almost all of the eighty downed flyers.

In the battle, one American battleship had been hit by a single bomb, and thirty-one U.S. planes had been knocked out of the sky. The Japanese lost three hundred forty-six planes and most of their navy. After "the Great Marianas Turkey Shoot" the Japanese kept a low profile on the sea, and they did not do much in the air for the remainder of the war.

The pilots of thirty-five of the planes limping home saw more than they'd bargained for in the Pacific twilight. Tearing toward them as they headed for Guam was something like a plane—a large, flying box. As the sun set to their left, they saw the Catalina.

Corrigan had refueled in New Guinea where he had had a few drops of John Barleycorn; then he'd pushed the Catalina toward Guam. The good plane shook. So did Corrigan. He wanted some Japs. The McKendrick fiasco had left him frustrated. The good guys always have to win. He considered himself one of the very best of the good guys, yet in the last seventy-two hours he hadn't been winning. As he came upon the Japanese squadron, Corrigan's blood pumped hard, his face broke into a smile, his voice into a song not really distinguishable from the sound of the engines. "Waltzing Matilda" never sounded like "Waltzing Matilda" out of Corrigan's mouth. Actually, nothing he ever sang sounded like music. But he invested each note with gusto anyway, especially before a battle.

The Jap flight commander could not hear Corrigan sing, and therefore, he did not know what he was missing. He could see the Catalina, however, and he was not sure just what he was looking at. He had never seen anything quite like it before on land or sea, certainly not in the air. Radio calls from his right wing did not reassure him either. Was this a flying boat? Quickly, he made the assumption that whatever one wanted to call the thing coming toward them, it definitely belonged to the enemy. He decided to shoot it down. With the odds at thirty-five to one who could lose? He should have asked Corrigan before doing anything rash.

On orders four Zeros broke off to engage the Catalina. They were surprised when she headed straight for the first one she saw.

"Stay right there, you Nipponese cocksucker, and I'll blow your yellow ass right back to Tokyo."

The Aussie, looking like a wild man, grasped the controls. Stripped to the waist, caked with sweat and dirt, against impossible odds, he felt great, alive. He opened fire and tore the first Zero in half, the bullets slicing it as if with a knife. The severed plane went into a tumbling dive.

"*Sayonara, Fujiyama.*" Corrigan loved to scream in the plane, to scream and to sing.

On his right a Zero was trying to level with him; another on the left was doing the same thing.

"Trying to get me in a sandwich, huh? Want to eat Corrigan between two slices of Jap. Fuck you."

He yanked back on the throttle. The great seaplane hung in the air for a moment, hesitated, then dropped like lead in the wind. At that second, both Zeros opened fire. Their own bullets tore into each other. Jap plane destroyed Jap plane. Corrigan saw the one on his right scream past, trailing smoke and fire.

"Dumb," said Corrigan out loud, shaking his head in mock concern, "very dumb." He pulled back hard on the stick and jammed the throttle forward. The Catalina roared back up. Before the Jap flight commander knew what had happened, Corrigan hovered over him. His sheer daring took the enemy by surprise for the maneuverability of Zeros compared favorably with that of any plane flying in the Pacific, whereas the Catalina's could only compare with that of Dumbo the Flying Elephant. Still, no one who sat behind a stick anywhere in the sky compared with Captain Corrigan.

His last bit of aeronautic acrobatics had put a fierce stress on the right wing and Corrigan felt the Catalina try to roll. He flew above the Jap squad, waiting for them to break and attack, always aware that trouble comes from the rear. The twilight worked in the Japs' favor, and given such overwhelming odds, they had more eyes to spot him. That thought only fueled Corrigan's enthusiasm. He banked away at a sharp angle and swung low, casually firing on and hitting the two Zeros flying at the furthest point west of the formation. Then he dived into the half-light and came around under the enemy flight.

All the time Corrigan laughed, laughed and planned even more outrageous stunts.

"Keep them guessing. Keep them guessing," he muttered to himself. "Never let them know. Never let them know." He wiped his forehead with a dirty arm.

As well as the Japanese flight commander could tell, he had lost three planes. The other thirty-two had been flying most of the day and sorely needed fuel. His pilots were willing themselves to stay awake. They had suffered an ignominious defeat. More than anything he wanted to get them home safely. Instead, he was being harassed by a maniac who flew something that did not look like a plane. He spit and cursed at the control panel of his plane. He decided to destroy this son of the enemy if he did nothing else, and he informed his second-in-command that he, personally, would eliminate this intruder from the sky. He ordered the squadron to return to base without him, save for one plane he instructed to remain by his side.

The other Zeros, save one, sped off toward Guam, believing that their flight commander would take care of this business.

Corrigan saw the squadron head north. He figured at least one other plane had to be after him. He had no idea that two planes intended to blow the Catalina out of the sky. Instinctively Corrigan changed position. He took the Catalina up, then banked to the right, losing speed. In the red glow of the sunset he saw one plane, then another flying below him. They had not anticipated his move. Had he stayed on course, he would have been dead. He now figured the two planes would split and loop over him, one from the front and the other from behind. Since anticipation is most of the game, despite a lame right wing and a lack of fuel, he took the Catalina even higher.

Sure enough, his two pursuers did exactly what he'd expected. Only they did not find Corrigan. Corrigan was lost in the clouds. The Jap squadron had disappeared. He came out of the clouds and bore down on the Zero nearest him.

The young Japanese pilot did not see Corrigan, but he felt his presence behind him. Each time the pilot tried to get above Corrigan the Aussie climbed still higher. After a whole day of flying and of skirting death, the Jap's body ached. Adrenaline kept it going. Nothing much had bothered him earlier, even fighting a sky full of Yanks. Then the Americans had outflown them. The Japanese Air Force had been all but destroyed. His chances of living until nightfall had seemed slim. He had kissed life goodbye several times in the past few hours. Yet he had not shown fear. At this exact moment, though, with a crazy plane in front of or behind him, above, below, everywhere at once—and with the sun sinking over the Pacific, his palms were wet and sweat broke out on his upper lip and forehead.

Corrigan fired up his twin 20-mm cannons and hit the Zero from behind. He first scored the tail, and from there the holes ran up the Zero's back tearing the plane in half the long way. Bullets in his neck and head the young pilot died, never having shown fear, and his plane went into a spin.

"Die! Die! Die!" Corrigan yelled. A feeling of satisfaction came over him. He had done something constructive. He had not felt this good about himself for days. For him, to kill was to live again! He broke into another chorus of "Waltzing Matilda."

His celebration did not last long. The Jap flight commander made a pass and strafed the right wing of the Catalina. Corrigan felt the great plane dip and roll. He realized at once what happened. His eyes filled with rage.

"O.K. I've been too easy on you guys," Corrigan muttered as he stabilized his plane. "Time to get tough."

The Jap would probably loop over, swing behind and then come up from below. Corrigan decided to surprise the man by looping with him. The flight commander passed in front of the Catalina's nose, quite definitely in the wrong position. Corrigan fired and missed. Both planes fell back.

Corrigan could not wait long. He had little petrol and a lame plane. Besides, caution and patience were not among his virtues. Only a minimally critical region of the right wing had beel damaged, and the mending job seemed to be holding. He would be able to keep the plane in the air, but not for long and not easily. He had to outcalculate that Jap.

"Let's get this shit over with," Corrigan hollered, but the sky did not respond. The sun had almost disappeared. He saw only shadows.

The Jap flight commander had slightly better vision. He had a bead on the Catalina. Moreover, he suspected that Corrigan was in trouble. He took his Zero up. He planned to stay way above Corrigan, to let Corrigan think he had returned to base, to make him worry. After a while, he would swoop down at top speed, when the Aussie least expected that, and open fire.

The plan worked well. Corrigan had to stay low because of the damage to his plane, but he couldn't wait for the Jap to make his move. Instead, he went looking for the man. Anyone else would have headed home, but Corrigan angrily roamed the sky.

Both planes were low on fuel. The sun had gone down completely, leaving only a glow in the sky. Now, the flight commander could barely see Corrigan. The time had come to strike. The Catalina seemed to be circling. The Jap made his move.

The flight commander knew he must get Corrigan in one pass. In order to do so he would have to reveal his position. Once he did that, Corrigan's odds went up.

Call it instinct, but Corrigan had the feeling something was about to happen. He decided to change his pattern. He dropped the Catalina and then brought her up and around. The turns made no sense. Corrigan performed them just to throw his attacker of guard.

The flight commander came in at top speed only to find Corrigan gone. He dipped down, then headed up again. But Corrigan had already seen him,

"Corrigan, you are one smart son-of-a-bitch," the Australian captain yelled out, and he turned the Catalina in the direction of the Zero.

The two planes hovered opposite each other in the sky, animals ready to charge. The Zero started in first. With the faster, more flexible plane the flight commander had the nominal advantage. Nonetheless,

Corrigan flew right at him. The flight commander had expected Corrigan to back off and go for him on a turn when he would be more vulnerable. He'd expected more cat-and-mouse. Instead, Corrigan turned the tables, became the aggressor. The Jap had not expected *that* at all.

When he got close enough not to miss, Corrigan opened fire. The flight commander hesitated an instant too long. Twenty-millimeter slugs ripped the nose of the Zero.

Corrigan let out the kind of cry heard most often at rodeos. A trace of smoke remained like a dark shadow in the sky. Corrigan took his hands from the throttle, grabbed a dirty rag from the cabin floor, and wiped his face.

"Corrigan," he said out loud. "You are the best fucking pilot in the air. You are the greatest thing to happen to a plane. You are . . ." His voice broke off. Words failed him.

He had little time to glory over his victory. He needed fuel, and the Catalina needed repair. Vella la Vella was too far away. In some ways landing there would have been ideal. That base had been established awhile, and he could have received the best help to fix the Catalina. He doubted, though, that very many people would still be there. The Rangers had been sent out. The Marines had moved up into the Marshalls and the Carolines. Seabees would hold Vella la Vella. General Thompson, Flagg, and all that group had probably moved somewhere else too. He checked his map with a flashlight. He might make it to Eniwetok. Hall Island and Namonuito were closer, but he did not know the setups on them.

He thought there might still be fighting. Eniwetok had fallen in February. He knew that for sure, but he imagined the way the Yanks worked they would already have that place pretty well set up. He would take his chances there.

He turned the Catalina east toward the Marshalls. The pull on the wing reminded him that the Japs had gotten him twice in the last few days, had tried to destroy his precious plane. He looked to his right. He could not see in the dark. He hoped the wing struts held. He hoped his pontoons stayed on. He hoped . . . He eased back on the throttle. Every time he thought of anything happening to the Catalina anger broke out all over his body. He took the dirty rag from the floor and gently wiped the control panel. One of the many tragedies of the war in the Pacific would be Corrigan's inability to win it single-handed.

Although the *Mako* had broken away from the Pacific Fleet to drop the Rangers on the east coast of Saipan, news of the Turkey Shoot had already reached them. Spirits ran high. They had routed the Japs. Tokyo lay just a little way ahead. Maybe the war did have an end after all.

Heinman had gathered his gear long before anyone else and sat around ready to go. Wilkins checked his weapons one more time. Contardo was talking and yelling at people the way he always did when he got excited. O'Connor pulled himself together somehow. The Rangers stood around in their compartment, waited, and got in each other's way.

"Japs are all over the island," McLeane said entering the small space. "Lieutenant Commander Henderson will take the ship in as close to shore as possible. We go in by water."

The men expected to be set ashore in rafts.

"Wet suits?" Heinman asked.

"Wet suits," McLeane said.

Without a word, all the Rangers began to change from fatigues and field dress into rubber. McLeane had already decided to tow the equipment himself. He began to collect everything O'Connor needed to blow up the world, Wilkins's extra few weapons and all the added clothes and food and paraphernalia the Rangers always took with them.

Commander Henderson stuck his head in the door. "We're ready."

"Give us a minute." Everyone stood around silent. A hush had fallen over the sub. McLeane took time to gather their gear together and to pull it into the corridor and over to the hatch through which they would climb before lowering themselves into the sea.

When the Rangers finally emerged, looking like strange animals that walked awkwardly on fins, members of the *Mako* crew came forward to shake hands. Swanson and Ensign Meskin said good-bye last. Swanson stuck out a fat paw and mumbled something about it having been a pleasure and everyone should get lucky.

"Listen, you guys, give 'em hell." Meskin smiled and grabbed each Ranger by the arm. He seemed genuinely sad to see them go. "We had a lot of fun."

Commander Henderson, fully recovered, hung in the background. While the Rangers took their leave

99

he went over to McLeane who was preoccupied with getting off the ship safely and efficiently.

"Major, I want to wish you luck and to thank you for pulling us out of hot water and for giving us something to take pride in again. You were something else back there."

McLeane, who did not really like open compliments and who always wanted to get on with business, just nodded and tried to smile.

"This is really not a bad ship, Major. The men have been through . . ." Henderson's voice trailed off. McLeane, Henderson had learned, did not want to hear excuses. He patted McLeane on the shoulder.

"O.K.," McLeane called out. "Let's get going."

The crew watched the Rangers climb up the hatch and, one by one, disappear silently into the dark Pacific night.

Chapter Nine

The island loomed ahead of the Rangers as they made their way through the water. They could hear activity in the distance. Every splash and ripple sounded like a crashing wave. McLeane thought he saw shadows along the shore, flickers of light in the sky. Even if he could not be sure, he knew the Japs were out there. No matter where they landed sooner or later a patrol would come along. Behind them, the *Mako* had already disappeared. His feet touched the sandy ocean bottom. Time to go to work, he thought.

The Rangers pulled themselves onto a beach that did not provide much cover. None of the usual dendiki palm or maomori crowded near the water. Instead, solitary banyans reached toward the sky, dark shadows against a lighter background. Clumps of marsh grass shot up here and there. Without a word the Rangers removed their frogman gear and moved in toward the foliage. They would have to go a few hundred dangerous yards before the geography would offer help.

O'Connor didn't care how many Japs had him in their rifle sights. As soon as he hit the shore, his seasickness went away. The worst time of his life had passed, and he had lived through it. He could use some sleep, but then he could always use some sleep.

Contardo's eyes scanned the horizon ahead of him. He managed to see everything without moving his head, a feat which always amazed the other Rangers. His small, wiry body tensed. He prowled like a cat.

Heinman and Wilkins flanked the others north and south. Wilkins held an M-1 carbine at his side. He strode upright, like a cowboy going through the main street of town, seemingly oblivious to the danger waiting in the darkness. Heinman had most of his mind on the native population of Saipan. An inability to remember indigenous tribal names bothered him. His thoughts wandered through a list of Micronesian words that might suggest what these people called themselves. Few things in this life annoyed Heinman more than forgetting.

McLeane struck out ahead. He could feel the others behind him, knew each one's position. A deadly accurate sense of direction informed him of the way to go to get to the Jap headquarters the Rangers had been sent to destroy. A photographic memory gave him a pretty good idea of the terrain they would face and where. He reached the edge of the island undergrowth and stopped.

Warm night air touched their bodies as they slipped into their fatigues and then outfitted themselves with special knives and pistols. Each man

102

carried an M-1 carbine and a .45 automatic. Wilkins also held onto an M-1 rifle complete with a telescopic sight which he did not like but which he was ordered to carry. They all stood motionless for a while and listened to the jungle sounds. McLeane clipped a couple of extra grenades onto his belt.

"You men stay here," he said. "I'm going to look around."

"Let me go with you, sir," said Heinman, who always had to be in the middle of the action.

"No." McLeane adjusted his gear for the final time while the others retied their shoes, loaded their weapons, peered into the darkness, and hovered on the balls of their feet. "The pass word is 'Dodgers.'"

"Any orders?" Heinman itched to do something.

"Get some sleep."

McLeane had decided not to push through blind. He had a general outline of the terrain, but he needed to know the particulars. He also had to know the exact whereabouts of some of the patrols out there. He did not want the four best marines in the Corps walking into an ambush that could have been avoided. Besides, the chances of knocking out the Jap headquarters would be better in the dark. The Rangers would need time. He did not want to start out too soon. His mind calculated busily, methodically, as the men watched him disappear into the jungle. They listened, but could barely hear him move through the foliage.

No one spoke. Everyone just stood, alert at the edge of the darkness. Finally, Heinman gestured them all together.

"You guys catch some winks. I'll stand guard."

"No," O'Connor objected. "You guys have been taking care of me. Now let me take care of you. I've been fucked up on that sub, but I ain't fucked up no more."

No one argued.

"I'll relieve you in a few hours." Heinman said.

The Rangers spread out, but not too far from one another. Each managed to find a log or a clump of shrubbery behind or under which he could get comfortable. As he stretched out, Heinman realized how tired he was and he wondered how McLeane, who had slept even less, stayed on his feet. The guy amazed him. Wilkins carved a cradle in the sand and fell asleep at once. Even Contardo found himself dozing once he was horizontal. He had a sudden vision of the USS *Princeton* looming up alongside of him. He shuddered. O'Connor hid, motionless, in the jungle palms and grass. He, too, had to fight to keep awake. He checked his .45, the grenades on his belt, his ammo. Then he ran his fingers through the sand to reassure himself that land was beneath his feet.

At about the same time the Rangers put ashore on the east coast of Saipan, Major Imamura, Lieutenant Colonel Seguchi and three hand-picked imperial commandos were set down on the west. General Sasaki had watched as they'd left headquarters. He'd refused to salute. When he could no longer see them, he spit on the floor, a very uncharacteristic gesture for a general. Maybe they would not return. The thought made him smile.

From the moment they had departed from the Huon Peninsula things went wrong for Imamura and his band of troublemakers. The plane, with Seguchi at the controls, had run into engine trouble just as they'd hit Saipan. They'd had to ditch it with half their equipment on board. This misfortune only served to inspire them, to make them even more determined to stop the Rangers.

Imamura had figured the Rangers would land where and when they did. He had also expected them to cut directly through the island, hit Japanese head-quarters as soon as possible, then leave the way they had come. They might meet resistance coming and going, but nothing to slow them down much. He had respect for what McLeane and his men could do. He planned to set out at once and cut off McLeane before he could get started. Unlike his American adversaries, he knew Saipan first-hand. He had been stationed there at the start of the war.

In friendly territory Imamura could establish radio contact with HQ. He had no fear of being intercepted. Only a fool would try to use electronic communication with so many of the enemy close. Imamura had many opinions about the Rangers, but he did not consider them fools. Once his presence was established on the island, he would be able to move more freely. But first Imamura would make sure that his men were fully equipped to move out. A half moon cast a dim glow over the night. With everything ready and everyone alert he cast a final glance north toward Tokyo. This would be the Rangers' last mission.

*   *   *

Not even Corrigan had any idea how the Catalina had managed to fly so far. The fuel gauge had long since read empty. He'd caught a tail wind blowing from west to east and had learned early in his career how to glide. Still, he seemed surprised when the great, awkward seaplane put down in friendly waters only a few miles off the coast of Eniwetok. He had radioed ahead. A couple of U.S. Navy PT boats stood ready to take him in and tow the Catalina ashore.

Once on land Corrigan turned his attention to repairing the Catalina's lame right wing. Seabees had overrun the island. They should have the materials and equipment he needed. This time he would do the job himself. He wanted no help. But first he wanted to shower, eat, and sleep. He had no desire to see or talk with anyone. The last few days had hardly been his best. His recent air skirmish had left him very unsatisfied. Even if he had downed four Jap Zeros all by himself, the rest of them had managed to get away. And the whole experience with McKendrick had soured him. Worse yet, these had been his own—Australians. He could not blame the Rangers for what had happened to the Catalina. He began to burn inside, slowly.

On the more northern Pacific islands, cover along the beaches is hard to find. Around Vella la Vella and Rabaul dendiki ferns and maomori lean over the water, and palm trees cluster just inside the water's edge, but here the shoreline was unprotected by foliage, for the most part. The usual jungle growth flourished further inland, and while the banyan trees reached higher there than anywhere else, they protected nothing.

Corrigan irritated the sailors who towed the Catalina. No place offered exactly what he wanted. The Catalina required full and perfect sanctuary. Corrigan needed a quiet cove in which to mend and revitalize his baby.

"This guy's a nut," muttered one member of the PT crew. "He talks about that thing like it was real."

"You never heard of him?" his shipmate asked. Both men looked over at the intense figure at the bow of their small boat.

Corrigan stood, fists clenched at his sides, eyes scanning the horizon, a breeze ruffling his thinning, brown hair. Occasionally he glanced back at his plane, his love. The sight of her lame right wing enraged him.

"Who is he?"

"That's Captain Corrigan."

The name meant nothing.

"He's the craziest flyer in the whole fucking war. You never heard of him?"

The first sailor shook his head.

"Well, that's him, and that's the Catalina."

Nothing registered.

"He's still nuts," came the reply.

Dawn had crept up, shedding light over the ocean. The boat had skirted half the island with the Catalina in tow.

"There," Corrigan called out suddenly. "Over there."

Sticking out into the water, as if detached from the rest of the island, was a finger of land overgrown with a profusion of green.

"Go around to the other side of that peninsula."

Corrigan pointed, and the boat turned slowly toward shore. All the while Corrigan kept one eye on his beloved Catalina.

Once they were close enough to land, three members of the PT boat's crew jumped out and pulled the plane under an arbor of wide palms and overly large ferns Corrigan could not identify. He made sure to secure the bow mooring line to the stump of a banyan tree that was standing alone, half covered by the tide. After pulling and tying several times, Corrigan felt reasonably sure that the Catalina would not float away. He waved the PT boat out of what he now considered his turf. The crew left happily. Something about Corrigan made them all nervous.

Corrigan took a closer look at the Catalina before heading inland to camp where he might take a shower, get something to eat, and find a cot on which to sleep. He also had to know exactly what would be needed to fix his plane. He would need welding gear. The Seabees should have that.

Because of the thick underbrush on this narrow strip of sand in the northernmost tip of Eniwetok, Corrigan had to actually cut his way off it. The fighting, which usually destroyed everything in its wake, had left that patch of the world unscathed. Under more casual circumstances, he might have enjoyed nature's beauty. At that moment, however, he had severe hunger pains. He hacked and hatcheted his way back to civilization, muttering about the Japs and swatting insects that wanted to feed on his arm.

He finally made it through all the leaves and branches and tufts of grass and hemp and broke into the open. He took a deep breath and headed south, first putting his knife in his boot, then wiping his face with a forearm that had been scratched and ripped by thorns and foliage. He found himself breathing deeply. Exhaustion had finally overtaken him. He would forgo eating and a shower. He just wanted to sleep.

The horizon showed no sign of life. He thought at least he might run into a patrol. Only a few months before Eniwetok had been the arena for one of the hardest fought battles of the war.

Enough light had come up to allow him to see well into the distance. He stopped to look again. He could not be sure, but he thought he could see something coming toward him. He drew his Owen to port-arms.

In the predawn light he could distinguish the clear outline of a jeep and the less clear outline of two figures in the front seat. He leveled his trusty Owen submachine gun at whatever was coming toward him.

"Put that thing down, Captain," a voice called out before the jeep even stopped.

Corrigan recognized the voice. A few feet from him a tall, leggy woman jumped onto the sand. Despite the dimness and the fact that she was wearing fatigues, he could see her body move. She belonged to McLeane. Just the thought threw Corrigan into a new fit.

"Hi, Margot," he sighed.

She extended her hand. He took it formally. His Owen hung at his side.

"I heard you had come in." They stood by the jeep. "You remember Major Flagg?" she gestured.

Corrigan nodded. He and McLeane agreed on at

least one matter. Neither had any use for Intelligence officers. Corrigan left Flagg with his hand open in greeting.

"We just got here ourselves," Margot put in quickly. "General Thompson decided to break camp at Vella la Vella and move closer to the northern Marianas."

No one spoke for a while.

"You know Mac's there right now," Margot said breaking the silence.

"I know." Corrigan wanted to sleep. "I guess I'll have to pick him up."

"That's the mission, Captain," Major Flagg chimed in, too cheerily to suit Corrigan who resisted the urge to make a snide remark.

"Just let me sleep and fix my plane," he muttered finally.

"General Thompson will give you your orders, Captain. You don't have to worry about that."

That moment may have been one of the few in Corrigan's life when he found himself too tired to slug somebody. He just closed his eyes and bounced along toward the center of camp while Flagg went on aimlessly. Exhaustion took over. For Corrigan the war would start again tomorrow.

Chapter Ten

Contardo lay on his carbine, dozing, hidden from the Pacific moon by the edge of the jungle. The handle of a bayonet stuck out over the top of his right boot. A .45 automatic hugged his hip. He hated wearing a helmet, but carried it with him anyway. He often used it as a pillow or a prop for his feet. That night he slept with his arms around it. His face wore a serene smile. In his head, the Brooklyn Dodgers had just taken the lead in the World Series. In his dream game of all dream games, Cookie Lavagetto's home run pushed the Dodgers ahead of the Yankees for the final time. The fans went wild. Vince Contardo, his nose blotting out the sky over Ebbetts Field, led the cheering. What a game! What a team! What a guy!

Wilkins and Heinman also slept. The boy from Georgia had conked out as soon as he'd stretched full length on the sand. He'd crossed his ankles, held his carbine across his stomach, and drifted off. Heinman had fought closing his eyes, but he, too, finally had succumbed. Neither of them dreamed.

Some yards away, hunched under areca palms, O'Connor fought to stay awake. The trip under water had taken more out of him than he wanted to admit. No one likes being sick. For O'Connor being sick also meant not doing his part, and he hated not doing his part more than he hated being sick. The jungle stillness did not help him war against sleep. He forced himself to listen for the slightest sound. The sound of the wind in the banyans felt like company. Banyans did not grow in Chicago. In Chicago they had plenty of wind, however. He tried to imagine Chicago. Only bars came to his mind. How many bars had he worked in? At that moment he could not remember individual bars. He remembered individual fights in bars and individuals fighting. He remembered Franklin the Goniff who tried to break a captain's chair over his back because he wouldn't serve Franklin anymore because the guy kept taking money which did not belong to him off the bar. He remembered Crazy Marge who'd thrown a beer mug at him. From two feet away she'd thrown the mug, one with a heavy glass bottom. She loved him with her life, she said as she hurled a heavy, glass beer mug a hair from his head into the mirror behind the Jack Daniels, green and black. He remembered that and how he'd had to belt the boss at one place the name of which he could not remember there in the jungle darkness so far away from anywhere that the number of miles made no sense to him. The boss had gotten drunk and molested the female patrons, which drove away business. He remembered fights and he wanted to go to sleep. O'Connor owed the others, he knew, for his lying around on the *Mako*, but he couldn't keep his eyes open. He wanted to, but he couldn't. Areca palms seemed to embrace him as his eyes closed. Wind rustled the banyan trees. O'Connor didn't hear it.

As McLeane suspected, a few hundred yards into the Saipan jungle the undergrowth got tough and gnarled. At first his feet slipped on knotted vines, then on island rock. His boots and legs took a beating as he made his way through the darkness. He wanted to get a clearer bead on Japanese headquarters before calling in the Rangers. All of them having to find their way at once could prove disastrous. He marked his direction and stayed alert to every jungle sound. The brush had changed. The lush greenery that grew nearer the coast gave way to brittle twigs and spiny branches that scratched his face. Still he moved quietly and swiftly straight ahead.

Then, for some reason he would never know, he stopped. Nothing had changed. He heard no unusual noise, saw only what the jungle had to offer at night. Still, he pulled up short and stood, carbine at his side, on the balls of his feet, ready to spring. He did not breathe. He thought he heard leaves rustle. Usually when animals go through brush, there is a slight sound of movement. He listened. He could feel the stillness. He moved.

Suddenly, the ground fell away and McLeane found himself falling into a pit that had been hidden, covered with branches and brush. Down he fell onto wet rocks. He landed on his back. Above him the night sky was only slightly less dark than the surrounding blackness. He still held his carbine. His .45 automatic was secure at his side. He checked his grenades, ammo, bayonet. Everything had remained in place. He had lost nothing, except his dignity and maybe his life.

Overhead he heard voices. The silhouettes of faces appeared over the edge. The pit could not have been more than ten feet deep. Sounds came down to him like so much chatter, as though an army of nervous monkeys had encircled him. He had torn his shirt in the fall, and his left shoulder, where he'd ripped his supraspinatus muscle on Hill 457, had started to throb.

The sounds faded, and a single voice called down to him. McLeane understood only enough to know the word "rope." Japanese, regrettably, was not in the core curriculum for liberal arts majors at Columbia. Upon his return to the U.S., he would see that such a flagrant omission was corrected. He felt a rope dangle on his head before he saw it. He figured his hosts wanted him to climb it. Using his right arm mostly and working footholds in the wall of the pit, McLeane managed to break out, to pull himself onto the clearing above. Japanese soldiers disarmed him immediately, none too gently, and tied his hands behind his back, again with less respect than he felt due him. He would remember that.

"You Amelican boy," came the announcement.

How brilliant! McLeane thought. Who would not appreciate brilliance at such a time? Identity, however, had never been one of his problems.

"Yeah, Amelican boy." He nodded.

McLeane could not tell much about his captors, how many there were or what they looked like. He just stood there, unable to go very far, while the Japanese jabbered away. Whatever they had on their minds, they expressed it with conviction. No one attempted to keep his voice down. They talked as though they owned the island.

The soldier who'd spoken earlier broke from the others, approached McLeane, and proceeded to scream at him. McLeane remained motionless. He could sense movement. The soldiers had made a circle around him.

The distant fire of Type 97s shattered the night. McLeane wondered how the Rangers were doing. He heard flak but no sound of any plane. Japanese surrounded him. Shrilly, the soldier continued to berate him. McLeane's eyes scanned the darkness. At ten o'clock a few yards away he sensed an opening in the shrubbery. Slowly, quietly, he worked his hands. He might loosen the rope that bound them, but that would take time. He had no idea what the noble son of Hirohito, standing in front of him was thinking or why he was yelling, and he did not care. He suspected, though, that sooner or later his Oriental hosts wanted to put a bullet through his brain. He also wondered how long it would be before he found out whether or not they intended to pull out his toenails first.

McLeane had spent the entire war on the balls of his feet, so when the rifle butt came at his head he was prepared and jumped away like a cat. A second blow to the other side of his skull also missed. He didn't wait for a third, but broke for the jungle, running with his hands still tied behind him. Those years of training on the Columbia football team, learning how to keep his balance, how not to fall down, at that moment counted more than anything else he'd ever known. He thanked Coach Lou Little for all the hours he'd spent running in and out of tires, sweat dripping down his legs and into his eyes.

The Japs, all of them, taken completely by surprise, waited an instant too long to respond. McLeane knew how to move through tropical foliage, better than any of them. In a flash, protected by the maomori and dendiki palm and the darkness, he disappeared.

He did not go far, however. Only yards from where the Japs had held him captive dense thickets of jungle bramble, a low wall covered with ferns and palms, stood in his path. Instinctively, he threw himself over and into the thorns and sharp branches that stuck up through the tangle. As sharp points and edges scratched and tore his arms and face, he settled into the angry mass. His heart pounded, his shoulder ached, his skin burned. While he waited for the Japs to find him, he struggled with his bonds. He rubbed his wrists against anything that seemed to cut. He worked his hands. His whole body, from his hair to the soles of his feet, hurt. He could feel the sticky wetness of blood where the ropes kept him from moving. He heard voices a few feet away on all sides. His pursuers did not seem happy.

McLeane hoped the rest of the war effort had more going for it at that moment than he had. The Marines should have made a move by now. He expected to hear the sound of battle in the background. Maybe they were having trouble. The Japanese still held the Marianas—their last outpost. Next came Tokyo. If they had fought hard before, they would be even tougher now. Voices called back and forth all around him. One false move and he could forget about the Marianas, the war, the Rangers. He figured it wouldn't be much longer before they started firing into the jungle indiscriminately.

Suddenly, his hands broke free. He flexed his fingers. His wrists and the palms of his hands had been badly torn. He had no weapons, not even a bayonet. The jungle around him seemed oddly quiet, and he suspected the patrol had moved ahead, though he could not think why unless they thought he had escaped. He tried to slip out of his bed of briars and head back to the coast where the Rangers waited for him. Then, maybe one hundred yards ahead, he heard Type 97s open up and an incessant barrage of 8-mm shells pounded the brush. They thought he had gone farther than he had.

McLeane freed himself from the thicket and, on his stomach, crawled in the direction from which he had come. In the dark, looking up, with ferns and dirt in his face, McLeane found the going rough. Also, north and east looked a lot alike. He wanted to get a few more yards between him and his captors before he made a run for it. He pushed ahead. Then he saw them, just outside his reach, pointing outward, two pairs of enemy boots.

McLeane didn't hesitate. Kicking off from the soft earth, he lunged for both Jap soldiers at once, bringing them down from behind. They never knew what

117

hit them. For that split second McLeane could have been back on the gridiron. But football players don't use guns, a consideration that did not escape McLeane. He easily wrested a weapon away from one soldier and smashed him convincingly on the back of the head. The man fell face forward in the dirt. Before the other Jap could level his automatic, McLeane, using his newly acquired piece like a baseball bat, clobbered him on the hand. The Jap let out a cry of pain. These guys were making too much noise. McLeane hadn't wanted to open fire and attract their buddies farther away in the jungle. He connected with a short punch to the stomach. The contact felt clean. The Jap went down. McLeane cracked his skull with the rifle butt. He wondered at that moment why Japs sometimes didn't wear helmets in combat. He cracked his skull again. They should wear helmets.

The weapon felt odd in his hand. The stock had an unusual shape, a short barrel. He was holding a 6.5-mm Type 11 submachine gun. The thing had to be twenty years old. He reached down and took ammo and a pistol from one of the bodies. The pistol, he could tell, had to be a Nambu. He knew about the Nambu. It was garbage. The Japs knew that better than he did. He wanted a piece of America in his hand. He wanted his .45 and his carbine back, and he would get them.

He would get them sooner than he expected. The Japs up front heard the noise and ran back. McLeane swiveled and fired into the night. He pounded them with bullets from the odd gun in his hand. They fell to the ground, groaning. When the ammo ran out he scrambled for cover to reload. Cover is easy to find in the night. Meanwhile, Japs were everywhere. It occurred to McLeane that these guys had never seen combat. They had been stuck out here waiting. McLeane had no idea how many there were, but he could take care of them all.

Having notified the Japanese staff that the Rangers might be on the island Imamura and his commandos moved through the Saipan jungle confidently. Though the going would be tough, his men knew the territory first-hand. McLeane's men did not. The terrain alone could kill them. Imamura smiled. After his humiliation at Vella la Vella, and after the Rangers had managed to blow Hill 457, no amount of pain and suffering would be enough for the Americans.

He would need help, however. He would need help from McLeane. McLeane would have to make a mistake—just one mistake. In reviewing the portfolio on the Rangers, Imamura had to admit he did not know what that mistake would be. For McLeane, on paper anyway, looked like the perfect commando leader. He had experience in virtually every aspect of military science. He had brains—lots of brains— courage, and strength. Most of all, his men followed him without question. For the briefest instant Imamura looked at his own men. They were tough and proven, but he did not know them well, and they had not worked much with each other. He wondered what mistake McLeane would make.

He led his commandos, with Colonel Seguchi,

toward headquarters. They moved quickly through the dense undergrowth. Imamura wanted the Rangers cut off. He wanted to take them by surprise. Colonel Seguchi felt the blood pounding stronger in his head than at any other time during the war. They all forged straight ahead into the night, hacking with their swords.

Chapter Eleven

Dawn broke and Contardo woke to find a Nambu pistol pointed at him. The other Rangers opened their eyes to the same greeting. A patrol of Japanese marines encircled them, silently watching, weapons ready. They did not move when the Rangers first stirred.

If none of the Rangers felt especially good about their predicament, O'Connor felt absolutely awful because he had allowed this to happen. He had only wanted to do his part after being sick, yet he couldn't remain alert enough. He looked up at three Japs who did not smile. The Rangers had been captured before but they had never been caught quite so flatfooted.

Heinman regarded himself with utter disgust. For at least one moment in his life he had failed as a pro. Wilkins just lay stretched out, shaking his head. McLeane, they knew, would be more disappointed than angry and would risk his life to save them from their own stupidity. Contardo saw the sun rise through the legs of a Japanese marine. Never one to get ulcers, he had enough stomach bile just then to corrode all of the Marianas. The Jap above him moved his weapon and said something. Contardo did not know what to make of it. He was annoyed.

"What's he saying, Adolph?" Contardo had no desire to do anything even slightly wrong.

"He wants you to get up." Heinman did not like delivering the message. "And I would suggest that you not try anything."

For a change nothing could have been further from the mind of the Flatbush Kid. The only ass he wanted to kick at that moment was his own.

"Why me?" he asked nobody in particular, getting up slowly from the sand.

"It's your nose," Wilkins called over. "They think it's a jungle animal, and they want to stuff it and send it to Tojo or whatever the fuck his name is."

Well, at least they were all together. That idea had never appealed to Contardo before, but now he could be thankful for small favors. He felt sand slip down his pants. He wanted to shake himself, but suppressed the urge. Instead he stood with his hands over his head while someone went to his right boot and removed the bayonet. They had already confiscated his other weapons. All he had left was his hands.

The other Rangers now moved to get up. Other Japs frisked them. To Contardo the Rangers all looked down in the dumps. He could count fourteen Japs. Most patrols run with twenty. Six of the enemy could be elsewhere, or, perhaps this patrol was short.

Contardo tried to think like McLeane. If the patrol

had only fourteen members, it probably did not expect to come across the Rangers. It had probably just been sent out on a routine reconnaissance mission. If it had gone out for something specific, a full complement would have been used. Perhaps, though, Rangers could expect to find six more Japs in the bushes. Contardo was able to get that far with his thinking. How McLeane always knew the difference still escaped him. Somehow, McLeane would know where the six guys were too. That really got Contardo. He assumed six bad guys were out in the bushes waiting, but he didn't feel smart about it.

The Japs lined up the four Rangers one behind the other, but did not bind their wrists or tie their ankles. Instead, the Rangers were made to march with their hands on their heads, a move which O'Connor found distinctly amateurish and which gave Heinman heart. The Rangers felt they might have been picked up by a bunch of novices.

"Do we look like the Marx Brothers?" Heinman threw out suddenly.

"We sure behaved like them," O'Connor fired back.

A Japanese soldier spoke. Whatever his exact words, the Rangers knew that the Japs did not like their talking. That high-pitched mumble meant "Shut up."

"Fuck them," came Contardo's immediate response. He began feeling like his old self again, and fucking the enemy was his standard solution for problems concerning the Japanese, officers in general, and all military Intelligence.

They entered the jungle like a safari, single file, one

behind the other. The dense shrubbery and high-growing palms cut out the early morning light. As they pushed onward, the undergrowth made walking harder, and without full use of their hands, the Rangers had difficulty negotiating the terrain.

After O'Connor had almost fallen twice, an idea hit him. He waited for the briefest clearing, then went down. The other Rangers followed suit. In a flash all four were on the ground, and just as fast they went for the nearest pair of Jap legs. They showed such perfect timing anyone would have thought the Rangers had choreographed the whole thing. The Japs had no idea what had happened. By the time the soldiers in front and behind had realized the Rangers had made a move it was too late. Eight of their own men lay on the jungle floor. The Rangers had taken their guns.

"Shit," Wilkins drawled, hardly out of breath. "This is like taking candy from a baby."

The Georgian easily stuck the body over him with its own knife and then held a Nambu at the ready, eager to fire it at the first little yellow face he could find.

An anxious flurry of bullets from one of the Japs at the rear of the line barely missed Heinman, but the son of Hirohito with whom Heinman, had been having a difference of opinion was mortally wounded. Normally, Heinman did not want his wrestling matches interrupted. Just then, however, he was grateful for the help. Flat on his back, Heinman locked onto another Jap. The soldier tried to fight back, but couldn't move his arms. Slowly, Heinman's choke-hold squeezed the life from the young Japanese. Heinman finished the man with a quick snap of the neck. The Jap's body fell on Heinman's chest.

As soon as he had a Jap in his hands, Contardo began to feel human again. His feeling of depression and self-abuse for having slept left him. He could only think of kicking yellow ass. He brought down one Jap with an ankle-high tackle. Another he dragged down by the back of his pants. In either hand Contardo had more strength than seven Japs. Neither Jap knew what had hit him when he landed on the soft jungle floor that was knotted with thick growth.

"I got both your fucking asses now," Contardo muttered. Even in the heat of battle he could not keep quiet.

The Jap who landed face-up took a hard fist squarely in the middle of his face.

"Home run!" Contardo always knew when he had connected. "You don't even know what a home run is you slant-eyed prick."

Contardo hit him again and knocked out all the man's upper teeth. Blood bubbled out of his mouth in a geyser. Contardo didn't hesitate a second, but reached over and grabbed the Jap's 6.5-mm Type 38 carbine and brought it down onto his forehead. The man's whole body just gave up with one shudder. All the while Contardo had the other soldier pinned, choking him with the heel of his boot. Every time the man moved Contardo gave him a shot in the larynx.

With one Jap dead he could turn all his attention to the other who was flapping around like a fish on land. Never one to make short work of a good killing unless absolutely necessary, Contardo often tried to use these last moments for instruction. Sometimes he would have victims recite the names of the Dodger infield. Sometimes, too, he would have them sing *The Star-Spangled Banner*. The present occasion, however, did not allow for education. Contardo found a bayonet hooked on the Jap's belt and plunged it through his sternum, smashing the bone on the way to the heart.

"Shit," Contardo let out under his breath. He had gotten blood on his hand.

Wilkins had disposed of two Japs right away by shooting them. No slouch with his fists, he still liked shooting them best, and that's what he did. He shot them. He took a service revolver away from one of them and very matter-of-factly blew his brains out while the other Jap, not quite sure what was going on, watched in stunned silence. Then Wilkins gave him his. The whole exercise took half a minute, so little time that Wilkins didn't really count this as part of the mission.

Then, Wilkins leveled a Jap carbine at the three remaining soldiers who headed the line of march. One bolted through the jungle. The others just froze, so overcome by fear they couldn't even swallow. Wilkins finished them with two bullets, swung around, and immediately dropped to one knee. Only the initial crack of Jap rifle fire could be heard before Wilkins opened up on the rear of the patrol. He simply cut them in half. They didn't even have time to make noise, but fell backward never to get up again. For Wilkins the whole incident proved very uneventful. He hadn't sweated. His pulse hadn't quickened. He just stood there and watched O'Connor take out his frustrations on one poor Jap who'd been beaten into the ground so badly he couldn't move.

O'Connor had his knees on the Jap's shoulders. He pummeled the yellow face with his fat fists again and again, shattering cheek bones, nose and temple.

"Hey, O'Connor," Wilkins suggested softly. "I think you got him."

A body next to the one O'Connor was working on stirred. Without breaking rhythm, as though he were using a punching bag, O'Connor gave the moving face a short, fast right.

"I'll get him." Wanting to be helpful, Wilkins raised his carbine.

"No," O'Connor hollered for the world to hear.

Wilkins lowered the carbine.

O'Connor went to work on both of them at the same time. His fists were numb and blood had splashed onto his wrists.

By that time, Heinman had come over.

"And the winner," he tried to raise O'Connor's hand, but O'Connor threatened to give him a shot too.

"No!"

Contardo appeared, slightly out of breath and fixing his pants leg. The three Rangers stood around while O'Connor's paws hammered what once used to be faces, but which in the last few minutes had taken on the appearance of pale red clay. All the while O'Connor whined under his breath. Each blow became more deliberate. Heinman saw tears running down the big Irishman's cheeks. The Rangers could only watch, until O'Connor, half dead himself from exertion, slumped, whimpered, and let his arms hang loose. Heinman and Wilkins pulled him up.

"Good job," Contardo offered, patting him on the back. "A clear decision. No doubt about it. The judges gave you every round."

O'Connor tried to collect himself.

"I'm sorry I fell asleep," he said finally. "I shouldn't have fallen asleep."

"We all fell asleep," said Heinman.

"We was all sleepy." Contardo had become known for introducing into every serious conversation the element of incontrovertible fact.

"Look, I was on guard. I fell asleep. And we could have got killed." O'Connor would not buy anyone else's version of what happened.

The Rangers took a few moments to gather their gear. Wilkins wanted his own automatic back. Since losing his favorite Smith and Wesson, he had gotten especially fussy about what he used to kill Japs. They let the bodies lie there and regrouped in the middle of the clearing.

"We had better get back to the beach and wait for Mac," Heinman said, tucking his shirt in for the fourteenth time.

Contardo had already started to move. O'Connor had trouble fastening a grenade. Wilkins, with the same eyes that shot squirrels in the backwoods of Georgia, glanced around the Saipan jungle.

"We better not go no place," he said in his typical flat voice.

For a second a strange hush fell over everything. Then the Rangers saw them, rifle barrels peeking through the maomori ferns and from behind the dendiki. They dropped their weapons, raised their hands, and waited.

McLeane did not count the dead around him. When the Jap Type 11 jammed, he threw it into the brush. By then, however, he could find only a couple of the enemy still moving. He surveyed the carnage and ran his hands over his face. His chest heaved. The trees and undergrowth were so thick the time could just as easily have been midnight as early dawn.

Suddenly, three Jap soldiers, wounded and half-crazed, came at him from the ground and knocked him down. His head hit a rock. McLeane lay stunned, and in that instant he got a heel in the face and another one in the gut. The wind went out of him. At that moment McLeane would have been finished except that one Jap tripped and fell across his chest. McLeane got the man in a choke hold as the others danced above them and tried to get at McLeane.

The Japanese were small. In hand-to-hand combat they could not compare in strength to the larger Americans, and McLeane was larger and stronger than most Americans. He whipped the Jap around like a rag doll, tossed him aside, and sprung to his feet facing his other adversaries.

Something happened to McLeane then. He had been fighting, putting his life on the line for the last half hour, for the last three years, and he had grown weary of it. He was suddenly tired of always being in the jungle, in the dark, fighting Japs or sharks or the weather. He wanted out. Rage welled up inside him.

He looked at the Japs opposite him. He looked at them, and he wanted their asses.

McLeane, usually so cool in the hottest situation, charged. He grabbed both men by their necks and smashed them together. Dazed, one Jap lunged at McLeane, head down and ready to ram him. McLeane chopped him on the back of the neck, brought a knee up into his face and threw him hard against the trunk of a banyan tree. The other soldier saw what had happened and started to run. McLeane dropped him at the knees with a tackle better than any he'd ever made for Columbia. The man spun around and with lightning speed kicked McLeane in the groin. The pain made McLeane want to throw up. He took a kick to the face. Blood ran down his nose and chin. McLeane grabbed the Jap's foot and flipped him. The Jap, hurt, came back too fast for McLeane grabbing him by the back of his neck. McLeane's life was being squeezed out of him. With one great effort he brought both elbows back into the soldier's ribs and stood up.

McLeane had had enough of flipping and kicking and choking. He wanted some good old American barroom brawling. He waited for the Jap to get up. His fists were ready. He wanted to take this guy out the way guys are supposed to be taken out. Standing, straight and craving the feel of bone on bone, McLeane hovered in front of the enemy. The two opponents made eye contact. Then McLeane saw the glint of a knife. This was not the fight he wanted, but it was a fight he knew how to win.

The Jap lunged at McLeane. McLeane grabbed his knife arm and twisted. The blade fell to the ground. It was too easy. He knew his enemy was tiring, tiring fast. These were not seasoned troops. McLeane swept up the knife. Even in the jungle darkness he could tell the Jap knew it was all over. He didn't even try to move, but put up his hands in self-defense. McLeane walked over and stuck the knife into the man's belly just under the rib cage and turned it. The Jap fell forward onto McLeane. McLeane stood there as the Jap slid down his body onto the bed of fern and dead palm. He felt sorry for the kid, but not sorry enough to let him live.

Give them even a little break, he thought, and they would come back to kill Contardo. However much he might want Contardo dead at times, he could not allow that.

He checked to make sure all the bodies were real corpses. The Jap he had thrown against the banyan tree had a broken neck. Nothing could have made McLeane happier. He searched the undergrowth for his weapons. He wanted his own automatic back and his own carbine. After some time, he found them. He had not done what he'd set out to do. The thought irritated him, but he did have to get back to the Rangers. He never worried about them in terms of fighting the enemy. They could take care of themselves. He worried about what they might do to each other if left alone too long. He headed back toward the coast.

Chapter Twelve

Japanese headquarters on Saipan sat in the middle of the island, covered by jungle ferns and palms and heavily guarded by rings of silent soldiers. The Rangers, their hands tied behind them, first set eyes on it in the noon sun that slanted through the banyan trees. These captors had bound them securely, and before entering the compound they were blind folded. How long or how far they walked no one could tell; they seemed to change directions so many times. No one spoke. Heinman tried to remember all the twists and turns. O'Connor returned to thinking he was responsible for what had happened again. Contardo just wanted to kick more yellow ass. Wilkins had to pee.

Once inside the small, bamboo stockade they could see daylight; it slipped through the spaces that surrounded them. Wilkins emptied his bladder immediately, even before Contardo spoke.

"I like the places they put you up in," he complained, looking around. "Even the marines can do better than this."

The Rangers barely had room to sit.

"Did you have to piss, Wilkins, inside this fucking dump?" O'Connor forgot how guilty he felt long enough to berate Wilkins. "You couldn't do it outside? Now we all got to sit in piss—your piss."

"I couldn't help it." Wilkins ignored the exaggeration. In fact, he had pissed very neatly in one corner, and he'd planned to sit in that corner anyway. True, a little had trickled into the center of the area, but not much, and the jungle growth covered it. Besides, war is hell. Wilkins decided not to mention that.

Heinman checked out the structure, pressing against the strips that held the bamboo together.

"Don't waste your time, Adolph," Contardo said. "What would you do after you got out? They've got one hundred guards out there for every one of us."

"I'll take those odds," O'Connor chimed in.

"Naturally," Heinman replied. "When did a hundred-to-one odds ever stop you?"

Contardo didn't say anything. They knew what he meant. They also knew he was right. For a long while no one spoke. Each man was trying to think of something appropriate to say.

"There," Wilkins said finally as he plopped to the floor. "I'm sitting in my own piss."

"If I knew you was going to get so upset, I wouldn't have said nothing." O'Connor had gone back to feeling bad again.

No one spoke about McLeane, but all of them wondered where he might be and what he might be doing. First, they had assumed, tacitly, that he was all right. Second, they knew he would come looking for them. Third, they half wished he wouldn't. Heinman stood up and tucked his shirt in again.

"You losing weight?" O'Connor had fully recovered from his bout of guilt.

"What do you care?" Contardo had to get into the act. "You his mother?"

"He just makes me nervous always getting up and fixing his fucking pants."

"Maybe I am losing a little weight." Heinman always had to be serious. He checked his waistband.

Anyone who knew the Rangers could see they were at it again. Had McLeane been there, he would have walked out and they would have known why. They realized they were back to their old games and decided to stop playing them. This situation demanded quiet. They moved to neutral corners and shut up. They said nothing for a long time.

On Eniwetok Corrigan couldn't sleep. He even walked back from camp to the Catalina to get a bottle of Aussie hootch. He lingered only a moment. It made him sad to see the Catalina gimpy and akilter. He would have to start a major repair job as soon as possible. If he could contact the commander of the Seabees, all the equipment he needed would be at his disposal, he was sure. Those guys were the salt of the earth. And this time he would fix the Catalina better than new. He wanted no more half-assed, make-do jobs. That wing should be solid and looking good. He gave the old plane the thumbs-up sign as he walked away, and he muttered about how much he loved her.

Still, what with the alcohol, exhaustion, light shining through the tent, and his anxiety over the Catalina, Corrigan could not sleep. Finally, he got up and, in the heat of a jungle afternoon, wandered around the camp so recently constructed on an island that, only months before, no one knew existed. He thought of taking another shower, but he had already taken two.

"There you are."

He heard a disembodied voice, one he did not know well, but one he remembered. He just stood still in the hot sun until the sound came closer.

"Corrigan, I've been looking all over for you." He remembered the voice. It belonged to Gen. Archibald Thompson, United States Marines. He preferred hearing other noises. But Eniwetok was small, and anyway, the two men did have business. He felt the general come up close behind him. Someone else was with him. Corrigan turned. Waves lapped up on the beach.

"Corrigan . . ."

The general stopped to salute. Corrigan didn't think people went through such formalities anymore. He saluted. He nodded toward Margot.

"Corrigan, there has been a change of plans." Thompson took Corrigan's arm and guided him along the hard sand by the water. Since he'd had no real idea of what the plans were to begin with, Corrigan really couldn't know how they had changed.

"I want you to get to Saipan as soon as possible." Thompson sounded urgent. More than ever Corrigan wanted to go to sleep. "I want you to go to Saipan and be ready when McLeane has to leave."

Corrigan quickened his step. However near exhaustion he may have been, he wanted to get away from Thompson. After McKendrick's folly, he could hardly complain about McLeane. Even though he could not blame the Americans for what had happened to the Catalina in the last two days, he would never get used to the way they wanted everything yesterday. What an arrogant, demanding bunch.

"You just tell me what you need, Corrigan." Thompson hustled to keep up. "I'll have it for you in twenty-four hours."

"I need sleep, General. I need twenty-four hours of sleep." Corrigan kept right on walking. "Can you get that for me?"

General Thompson chose to ignore the sarcasm. "What else do you need?"

Corrigan stopped short.

"I need a new wing for the Catalina. And I need that bad. Otherwise nobody's going anywhere, General." He emphasized the point by staring straight at Thompson, then turning and leaving abruptly.

"You've got it, Captain." Thompson did not bother to follow. He just nodded and watched the Australian go off.

Within the hour a platoon of Seabees had set to work putting the Catalina in order. They used the best materials available. For a change the great plane got repaired with real metal and real bolts and nuts—even real solder held everything together. Professional welders did a first-rate job that Thompson himself proudly supervised. He stood on the edge of the beach with his hands behind his back and nodded approval. He knew only that airplanes went up and came down, nothing about how they should be fixed. Margot, who knew even less, watched with him. They both stood by the arbor of jungle palms and smiled while teams of repairmen scurried, like ants, all over the wing of the Catalina.

Meanwhile, Corrigan slept in fits and starts. The shower did him good, but the alcohol soured his stomach and gave him a headache and bad dreams. No matter how he turned on the fold-up cot in the BOQ to which he'd been assigned, he could not get comfortable. Finally, grumbling all the time, he put on his shoes and headed out toward the Catalina. He knew he could sleep there.

From a distance he could see the commotion around his plane. The thought of anyone else fussing over his baby drove him into seizures. Overcome by an uncontrollable anger, Corrigan broke into a dead run.

"Hey! Hey! Get off my plane." Corrigan turned red in the face and waved his arms. "Did you hear me?"

General Thompson looked around to see a furious Corrigan coming toward him.

"Did you authorize this, General?"

"Well, Captain, you said you needed a new wing, and we have to get to—"

"I'll get my own new wing, damn it. That's my plane, and nobody gets on it but me." Corrigan had moved within inches of Thompson's face.

"Captain, do realize . . ." But Corrigan wasn't

listening. He had already begun throwing people off the Catalina. Almost at once the hard-working Seabees stopped what they were doing and ran to shore, as far as possible from the mad Australian.

"He's crazy, sir," said one out-of-breath Seabee to General Thompson.

"I know."

From the wing of the Catalina Corrigan stopped screaming at everyone long enough to look over the work the men had done on his plane.

General Thompson, who was familiar with Corrigan's reputation and behavior, turned to Margot.

"Why don't you try to talk some sense into him?" he asked.

Margot shrugged. The men all saw her move along the sand in the direction of the water. She took off her hat and let her long, red hair hang loose in the bright Pacific sun.

No one could hear what she said, but before long she returned.

"He's calmed down," Margot told General Thompson as she put her fatigue hat back on her head. "I told him it was either working with our guys or with the British." Corrigan hated the British.

At Thompson's signal the men swarmed onto the plane. However anxious they may have been to get to work again, they kept a cautious, respectful distance from Corrigan, who barked out orders like a drill sergeant.

In the middle of everything Corrigan could not resist glancing toward Margot. She looked sultry even walking on the sand, her hips rolling, her hair down. Her breasts under the loose-fitting fatigue blouse did not go unnoticed. She was a stunning woman, and he was lonely. The combination renewed his intense dislike for McLeane, the lucky bastard.

Major Imamura and his band reported to headquarters, establishing their presence on the island. The Japanese command there did not seem impressed with them or their mission. One of their own patrols had already picked up four Rangers. Imamura got the cold shoulder. He did learn, however, that McLeane remained at large. He intended to regain much of his lost prestige by capturing the elusive American major.

That same elusive American major had decided to find out what had happened to his men. He stood on the beach, in the open, at the spot where he had left the Fearsome Foursome. He could tell from the remaining footprints swept by the ocean breeze that they had had company. He figured it was a patrol rather than a party of three of four. He also knew his men had been taken by surprise since he could see no sign of a struggle. On the one hand, he'd never seriously entertained the thought that they might be in any real danger. On the other, he knew he had to free them.

He followed a beaten opening in the jungle brush, walking on sand through the undergrowth. Dendiki palm and ferns had been hacked at with swords. McLeane could see the thin, clean cuts. They had walked through single file. He saw no signs of a struggle. He waited to come upon the first clearing. If he knew the Rangers at all, the action would start the moment they had room.

In time he came upon a clearing. Clearly, a struggle had ensued. The Rangers had won, he could tell. He also realized they'd managed to get themselves recaptured. Outside the open area, he noticed trampled brush. Japs had surrounded the Rangers. They'd fought off one patrol only to be captured by another. For a moment McLeane tried to reconstruct what might have happened. He smiled. It had taken two patrols to capture four Rangers. He had a happy vision of Contardo on top of some unsuspecting Jap soldier and of Heinman sending out a flying kick to the teeth. Wilkins probably had sat calmly wherever he happened to be and cleanly picked off this or that Jap. O'Connor, without doubt, had taken his fists to some poor face pulverizing otherwise interesting cheekbones into soy meal. McLeane wondered why the Japs had taken them alive. From the enemy's point of view they all deserved to be shot. McLeane figured that someone wanted them, knew who they were and wanted them. That meant they also knew who *he* was and wanted him. The Rangers' mission had been to knock out Jap headquarters and clear the island of pocket resistance. Their immediate challenge might be just keeping alive. McLeane did not smile.

Chapter Thirteen

"What the fuck are we doing here? Does anybody know?" Close quarters and bad air had gotten to Contardo. "Why did they send us here? I mean what are we supposed to do?"

No one answered.

"I mean were we supposed to just take a boat ride underwater, fall asleep, and get caught by Japs? Is that why they sent us to this shithole? Did they send us to this shithole just to sit in it?"

"They sent us to 'this shithole' to eliminate enemy headquarters and rid the island of guerrilla resistance," Heinman volunteered.

"Oh, thank you, Mr. Know-It-All." Contardo wanted to get up and move, to stretch and run, to shout—wanted to do all the things confinement in a six-by-eight pen made impossible. "'Guerrilla resistance.' What the fuck is 'guerrilla resistance?' How come when you start to know so much you always end up talking like a fairy?"

Contardo proceeded to talk in a falsetto about ridding the island of 'guerrilla resistance.' He made mincing gestures with his hands.

"Jealousy is unbecoming." Heinman knew Contardo too well. Contardo was strung out.

"Jealous? Of what? Of you?"

"Well, first of all you can't remember anything. Take our mission here. You can't remember why we were sent. Second, you don't understand whole sentences. If anyone speaks English to you with a subject and verb, you look at him as though he were talking Urdu." Heinman suppressed a smile.

"Yeah, I noticed that Urdu shit myself," chimed in O'Connor.

"The subject-verb riles you up, too," added Wilkins. "We've been talking about that among ourselves for a long time, about the subject-verb and how you get all jealous when you hear it."

Contardo understood the game at once and kept his mouth shut. He would find other ways to retaliate. But now the Rangers were doing what they enjoyed even more than fighting; they were having fun. They were not about to let a good thing go.

"I've only heard Contardo speak one complete, correct sentence in all the time I've known him," Heinman continued.

"You know, Adolph, I think you're right." O'Connor picked up the ball.

"Yeah, just one," added Wilkins who had absolutely no idea what was going on except that Contardo didn't like it.

"Fuck you!" Contardo emphasized his message

with a little nonverbal communication involving the middle finger of his right hand.

"That's it," Heinman pointed with mock excitement. "That's the sentence. He says that very well. What do you think, men? Have you ever seen such eloquence?"

"Beautiful, how he says that," O'Connor agreed. "And also very sweet and nice."

"Yeah, he says that real well." Wilkins was having fun. "Do you think he'd say it again for us, Adolph?"

"Yeah," O'Connor kept it up. "But the whole thing all over again. Not just part of it. Go ahead and ask him."

"Contardo, the guys here asked me to ask you to say your whole sentence again. They're impressed with the kind of product the Brooklyn public school system turns out. But before you say it give us a few minutes to collect ourselves."

The three Rangers straightened up and sat attentively as though ready to listen to Kreisler play the violin.

"We're ready, Vince. Give us the whole sentence."

Contardo tried to push a bubble of gas into the air, but his bowels wouldn't work for him. Instead, he simply scrunched himself into a ball and, with typical lack of grace, turned his face to the bamboo wall. The Rangers laughed.

As evening came, shadows fell over the island of Saipan. Imamura, followed by his men, moved through the jungle in the half-light, obsessed. Hacking fiercely left and right at anything in his way, he walked upright, like a man who owned the ground beneath his feet. His commandos walked with more caution, flanking him on both sides, keeping low and alert. Imamura was very conscious of his anger. He wanted McLeane, and he wanted him badly.

As for McLeane, he wanted to find his Rangers just as badly as Imamura wanted to find him. He could only guess where they might be. Meanwhile, his mind totally occupied with locating his men, he did not suspect that Imamura and a posse of Japan's most skilled killers had been sent to capture him. He, too, was alert for signs of the enemy's presence as well as signs of the Rangers. Signs of the enemy lurked behind every palm. He had to assume that the Rangers had been taken captive and were being held at Japanese headquarters.

Since Imamura knew what to look for, he had the advantage. He also had a reasonable idea of where to look. Given the American offensive to the south, the Rangers would have landed somewhere in the middle of the coast. That part of the island offered few hospitable spots on which to drop troops either by plane or ship. If Imamura headed directly toward the shore from headquarters, he would cover a lot of the ground McLeane would have to take to reach the Jap HQ. For Imamura, locating McLeane was a matter of time. Meanwhile he avoided the Japanese jungle patrols. McLeane had to destroy any Japanese he came across. Imamura had to keep from being destroyed.

Without realizing it, the two men moved slowly toward one another.

*   *   *

146

Contardo could no longer stand being cooped up in the bamboo pen that held the Rangers prisoner. He wanted to get out. He peered through the openings in the wall and into the surrounding jungle. Oddly, now the camp did not seem heavily guarded. He saw only a couple of figures in the dusk. He remembered the rings of soldiers that had first surrounded the compound. The High Command must be pretty sure of this stockade, Contardo thought. They had to be assuming that no one could get out.

"When do we eat around here?" Contardo had an idea.

"Who said we do?" Actually, O'Connor had no interest in food.

"What's on your mind, Contardo?" Heinman asked.

"I bet we can bust out of this place."

"Why don't we blow it down, huff and puff?" O'Connor, said. "Just like the three bears."

"How do you want to do it?" Heinman ignored O'Connor.

"They come in with the food. We jump them and split."

Wilkins had fallen asleep and had begun to snore. Heinman considered the prospect of breaking free. As Marines, they were obliged to escape at any possible opportunity. As Rangers, their reputation depended on their doing so.

"Suppose we don't get to eat," Heinman said finally. "And don't forget we've got to get out of the compound."

"Don't worry. I'll get somebody in here." On the first score Contardo seemed confident. "And we'll get out of the compound. We're Rangers. That's why

Uncle Sam pays us these high salaries."

"But there are a lot of troops out there." O'Connor said. "There may not be too many right outside here, but there's a hell of a lot someplace."

"He's right, Contardo. We need a better plan. If we just find ourselves out there with all those Japs to kill and no place to go, we're dead."

"Count me in." Wilkins opened one eye, then went back to dozing.

Reluctantly, Heinman agreed to do something. What exactly, he did not know. O'Connor decided he would just have to go along.

Contardo had neither the mind nor the patience for detailed strategy. He wanted to get out. "Look," he said, "I'll make a racket in a few minutes. We'll get someone in here. We'll jump him; then instead of heading back to where we came from, we'll go for the HQ."

"Yeah, and what do we do there?" O'Connor didn't believe in any of Contardo's plans.

"We take it. They won't be expecting us." Contardo was becoming impatient. "We were sent here to knock it out anyway. What's the difference? The Old Man isn't here. That's all."

Normally this line of reasoning would have sufficed. They would have agreed. The discussion continued, however, with Contardo driving harder to make his point. Finally, weary of talk the Rangers decided to go along with him. Contardo would wait awhile and then make noise. The Japs would send someone to investigate. The Rangers could be relied upon to do the rest. Contardo felt the blood pounding in his veins. At least he wouldn't be sitting

148

around. It never entered his mind that he or any of the Rangers might die.

Corrigan set the repaired Catalina down in the same cove where the Rangers had landed earlier. He camouflaged her with jungle green, checked his Owen, his bayonet—like the Rangers, he carried it in his boot—put another automatic in his belt to match the one already in his holster, gathered a handful of extra ammo and a couple grenades, and headed into the jungle.

Heading into the jungle at this point had not been part of General Thompson's perfect plan for Corrigan. That plan required Corrigan to sit and wait until the Rangers had finished their mission. They would return like homing pigeons, Thompson assumed, to the spot from which they had taken off. With Japs all over the island Corrigan couldn't use a radio. He felt Thompson's plan only made him a nonmoving target for any patrol that came along the beach.

Corrigan's style had always been a good offense. *His* plan required him to find the Rangers, and he knew the general direction of Jap headquarters. The birds had fallen silent. The heavy air stuck to his face, hands, and arms. Near the water there had been a breeze, but a few feet into the jungle nothing moved and dark came early under the banyan trees. Corrigan would soon have to use his night eyes. He stopped. Every sound in the jungle stillness mattered. He was alert, not only for enemy soldiers, but also for snakes, wild boar, and poisonous lizards, the enemies of all men.

He heard a rustle and reached slowly into his boot. He could not tell exactly what had made the sound or where it had come from, but he would be ready when he heard it again. He held his breath. Ahead of him and to his right at one o'clock about five yards away, the ground moved. A boa slithered toward the thick stalk of a high-reaching maomori. Once on the maomori, the snake would be at eye level with Corrigan, able to lean over and grab him by the shoulders.

Corrigan knew a little about boas. He'd had one for lunch once. It had held him in a crushing lock around the chest. He could only kill the thing by chewing through its skull. He recalled the taste of boa brains, the feel of splintered boa cranium in his mouth, and the smell of blood—and he got mad.

Out of the corner of his eye he could see the slimy bastard slither up and coil along under leaves. Corrigan hated snakes, and of all snakes he hated boas the most. They were not as fast as cobras or rattlers, but once they wrapped themselves around the body of their pray, the victim could look forward to permanent nighttime.

Barely moving his right arm, Corrigan brought the bayonet into position. He would have preferred to strafe the ugly scum with his Owen. That, however, would have made too much noise. His knife had never been his favorite weapon, but one did what one had to do.

He lunged. He missed, but recovering in a split second, he nailed the boa with his second stroke. The animal did not die. Corrigan watched it struggle for a moment. There was no real reason to kill the beast.

150

Actually, he enjoyed watching it struggle. But he needed his bayonet. No one can strangle a boa. In the dimness he could see the pinned animal flash its tongue. He wanted to crush its head. He felt a rock beneath his foot. As he'd moved further into the jungle the land had become rockier. He collected two palm-size stones. The snake remained tacked to the fat fern stalk. Corrigan looked at it. He could not see the snake's markings, only the outline of its head and a kind of shadow when its tongue shot out and a sheen glistened off its skin.

In one quick move he brought both hands together, smashing the boa at its eyes. He did the same thing again. The contact felt good. The feel of squashed snake meat did something for his spirit. He gave the boa another whack for good measure. The snake just hung, fastened by his bayonet to the mao-mori. A rush of great relief came over Corrigan. He had settled a score with nature. He wiped the bayonet on his pants and stuck it back in his boot. He straightened up, took a deep breath, and moved forward. The new, improved Corrigan was now about to take on the Japanese army.

Chapter Fourteen

Contardo's plan did not work. Worse, it had had no chance from the beginning. Contardo no sooner made a racket than a half-dozen Japs stormed the prison pen and pulled out the Flatbush Kid by his collar. They threw him to the ground and hogtied him like a baby calf. Bent and twisted, he was slung over a pole and carried, like a piece of meat, toward headquarters. None of the Rangers knew what had hit them. They sat motionless, staring at four Type 97s as the sound of Contardo yelling about "yellow cocksuckers" faded in the distance.

Contardo refused to shut up. He hated being penned in, but he hated being tied up even more. He did everything possible to bounce along the shaft on which he was carried, and he hollered without letup.

"I'll get you fuckers." He wondered if all the blood rushing to his head would cause him to pass out. "I'll kick your fucking, slanty asses, you—"

He never finished the thought. The butt of a 97 caught him squarely behind the ear. He later became conscious in an underground room, with the sorest head he could remember. Blood caked his wound and hardened on his neck. He wanted to touch it, but his hands were tied. The sour smell of jungle rot made him slightly sick. The warm dampness of the floor had soaked through his clothes. More annoying than that, O'Connor had been right: He had violated McLeane's Second Law of Strategy: never do anything in haste unless the enemy is about to claim an important life, and only then if you can't think of doing anything better. So much for being a leader. But Contardo did not learn basic things easily or quickly. He wondered how long he would have to wait for the Japs next move.

Not long. A door opened and four arms pulled him into the light of a larger room. His eyes took a minute to adjust. A kerosene lamp burned on a low table. The table may have been a box. Contardo could not see clearly. Uniformed figures stood in the shadows. A high-ranking officer stepped into the glowing circle. He might have been a general; Contardo could not tell. This officer held a swagger stick which he periodically slapped into his palm. A woman in oversized Jap fatigues stood beside him. She did not move. Contardo had no way of determining her rank. She had a plain Oriental face. No one spoke, not even Contardo. Two men went behind him. Another two flanked his sides. He could see them out of the corners of his eyes. There were many weapons in the room. He could hear boots click and scuff the floor, which was made of some kind of wood. The walls were constructed of bamboo, and looking at them, Contardo got the feeling of openness. He could hear his own breathing.

The officer who might have been a general slapped his swagger stick into his palm and spoke to Contardo, his voice brassy staccato that sounded like a toy machine gun.

"You are a Ranger of McLeane," the woman interpreted.

A Ranger of McLeane, Contardo repeated in his head. He figured this conversation would take a long time.

"Why have you come, and what is the American plan of attack?"

He had just begun to imagine that this woman whom he'd first seen only moments before wanted him. The disappointments one encounters even in the jungle. Contardo did not bother with his name, rank, and serial number. The officer spoke again, and then the woman. She repeated the questions. When Contardo did not answer, he felt a whip come down across his back. It cut into his flesh with a searing pain. He did not blink. The officer took another tack.

"Who are you? What is your name? What is your rank? What is your serial number?"

"My name is Leo Durocher. I am the greatest manager in baseball. You are a flat-nose twat."

He felt the whip twice that time. But such treatment would never make Contardo talk. His threshold for pain had never been fully tested. In the back of his mind he knew the Japs were only beginning. They had other ways to make him talk. He would cross those bamboo bridges when he came to them.

"Who are you? What is your name? What is your rank? What is your serial number?"

"My name is Leo—"

At a nod from the officer the whip came down twice more, this time across Contardo's face and chest. The pain annoyed him only slightly more, but the potential danger to his eyes provoked anxiety, and for Contardo anxiety always led to anger. Contardo, who had seldom been able to restrain anger, touched a new dimension of himself by not uttering a sound. At that point the officer left the room, only to return a few minutes later with the same questions but a new way of getting the answers. The man who followed the officer into the room walked directly to where Contardo sat and immediately removed his shoes. Contardo could not remember if the well-known water torture was Chinese or Japanese. Whichever, he had a funny feeling this wasn't it. Whatever this was he was sure he would not like it. He took a close look at the man who'd removed his shoes.

The officer's interrogation continued. This time, however, when Contardo refused to respond or to respond reasonably, the man drove a sliver of wood between his nail and his toe. Contardo wanted to kick out, but his legs had been strapped. He screamed loudly enough to wake the gods. For good measure the whip came down across his back and chest again, and the interrogation went on.

Contardo gave them nothing, not even his name. Having driven strips of wood into all of Contardo's toes, the man set them on fire. Contardo had never even imagined such pain, and he hollered himself hoarse until he passed out, fire still cooking his toes.

Imamura's commandos spied McLeane before he even knew they were on the island. Colonel Seguchi had taken the left-most flank. He moved northeast across the jungle a little ahead of the rest, creeping through the brush, silent and lizardlike, until he heard movement on the other side of the areca palm directly ahead of him in the night. A solitary American stood poised, waiting for the slightest sound. An M-1 carbine dangled at the end of his left arm. Seguchi scrutinized the figure in front of him. In the dim light something about the man frightened Seguchi. At the same time he felt pure admiration for him. Alone in a jungle he could not possibly know, with the enemy all around, McLeane had the presence of a great jungle animal. With one shot Seguchi could have brought McLeane down, but Imamura wanted him alive. Seguchi moved to get a closer look.

As the evening shadows deepened, McLeane's hearing became more acute. He was in trouble, just how much he could not know, but something or someone hovered out there. He also sensed movement. A whole patrol would have made more noise. He listened, waited, then turned slowly, dropped suddenly and opened fire, spraying 6.5-mm shells along a 180-degree arc.

Imamura knew at once what had happened. Seguchi cut a wide berth around the trapped Yank. Imamura wanted him. The other commandos crept in on their bellies. Imamura wanted McLeane alive, but he would be lucky to get him at all.

McLeane had set his square, American jaw. Who-ever-they-were had him in a trap. He had been ambushed. He didn't like the idea, but under these circumstances such occurrences were hard to avoid. He laid down another arc of shells with no result. He might have been able to bolt through the jungle behind him and get away, but the thought of running offended his sense of honor. He knew that if he sat long enough they would tip their hand. That would at least give him something to shoot at.

The Japs fanned around McLeane to cut down his chances of escape. Imamura stood back, waited for his men to get in position, then flung a stone across the clearing behind McLeane. McLeane turned and fired. He realized his mistake at once. He had fallen for the oldest trick in the book, one he'd known from the age of ten when he'd played cowboys and Indians. He had no sooner made his move than Imamura's commandos made theirs. The three who'd lain ready in front of him jumped his back. Seguchi, on the other side, waited.

McLeane, already annoyed at being ambushed, became angry when tricked. But he kept his cool. His first principle of strategy was never to act out of anger. He had three killers on him, and he had to work methodically to make sure he won and they lost. In the first few seconds of fighting he noticed something unusual. They had not tried to put him away. They could have knifed him easily or blown his head off. Instead, they chose to engage in hand-to-hand combat. Did they know who he was, and did they want him alive? If so, that would be one factor on his side. The Rangers never took prisoners. But who wanted him alive and why?

One Jap had thrown McLeane to the ground. Another had his legs. A third went for his stomach. McLeane grabbed the one at his head by the neck and threw him on the other two. The force stunned all three Japs. They knew now they were dealing with a man of mammoth strength. When they turned, McLeane was on his feet. His eyes moved from one to the other, then back across their faces. Each had drawn a knife. McLeane could not afford the instant needed to pull out his own. Barehanded and alone, he faced them. Anything could be coming at his back, but he would have to take that chance.

One Jap threw a flying kick which missed completely. Another, like a bull, went for his stomach. McLeane, stepped aside like a toreador, catching the edge of the blade across his abdomen and ending up with a surface cut above his navel. He went for the third. The Jap tried to stop him with a karate chop. McLeane caught his arm and flipped him in the air like a rag doll. As soon as he hit the ground, McLeane was on him. The Jap, stunned, couldn't move. McLeane grabbed him by the throat. Out of the corner of his eye he saw something coming at him. With one hand up to ward off any blows from the side, he choked the life out of the Jap under his thumb. His huge hands fixed in a steel grip, pressing on the man's windpipe and cutting off his breath. The soldier's tongue came out, his eyes rolled, his arms flopped, and his legs flailed, but McLeane had him out in seconds. Then a terrific blow to the back of McLeane's head sent him flying into a clump of palm. His senses registered excruciating pain and the distinct, nutty odor of areca. He started to rise.

In an instant the other two Japs were on him. Imamura and Seguchi both watched from opposite sides of the clearing and waited for their moment. McLeane didn't even seem winded, a consideration which did not please them. Half upright at first, then flying through the air, McLeane kicked a Nambu automatic out of one Jap's hand. The plans to take him alive had obviously been called off. The other Jap tried to fire on McLeane, but his weapon jammed. McLeane came up at him from the ground with the hardest right in the history of unarmed combat. The Jap reeled backward, then collapsed in a heap. McLeane pulled his .45 and wasted him with one shot through the head. Giving a quick paean of thanks to superior American technology, McLeane threw himself on the other Jap. Three-to-one against McLeane was almost fair. One-on-one, the Jap had no chance.

Still, the man fought. The Jap landed a boot in McLeane's gut and McLeane fell back with his knees up. The Jap came at him with a knife. The knife tore into his left shoulder, the same shoulder that had been so badly injured taking Hill 457. His vision blurred. He rolled away into the thick areca palms. The Jap went after him. He saw the blade come down and stopped the arm holding it. The two men struggled. The Jap went for McLeane's eyes. McLeane twisted free, landed on top of the soldier who now lay on his stomach. McLeane pushed the man's face into the jungle earth, holding his shoulders down with his knees.

At that moment Seguchi attacked from behind, screaming and hurling himself at the now-tiring American like a man gone mad. McLeane ended the misery of the Jap beneath him with a quick punch to the back of the neck. Seguchi would be another matter. He found it harder to ignore the pain in his arm. Seguchi was strangling him and calling him a "Yankee pig-dog" at the top of his lungs.

McLeane had already taken three japs, one hung on his back, and McLeane wondered how many more lurked in the jungle shadows. He brought his good elbow back into the lower stomach of his tormentor. Seguchi fell away. Both men stopped fighting to collect their bearings. They stood opposite each other and moved in a circle, working their hands like two wrestlers ready to go at each other. Seguchi lunged first, going for McLeane's knees and missing. McLeane seized his chance and brought a boot into the Jap's face. Blood poured out of Seguchi's nose and mouth. McLeane kicked him again. The Jap got up, spitting out teeth, and stood unsteadily like a fighter about to go down for the count. McLeane went right for him. Seguchi still held his knife, but couldn't use it. He only made slow gestures in the air, wide of the mark and weak. McLeane caught him with a hard right to the solar plexus. The knife fell. Seguchi doubled over. McLeane picked up the knife and stabbed the Japanese lieutenant colonel in the back of the neck.

That very instant, McLeane felt an unbearable burning race through the back of his left shoulder. He turned and fell to the ground. A Japanese soldier, unusually tall for his race, stood over McLeane. He smiled. He held a bloody bayonet.

"Please don't try anything, Major."

The perfect English did not take McLeane by surprise.

"Major Imamura, I presume."

Imamura did not answer. He had his man.

Contardo came to, screaming with agony from the pain in his foot. The solitary light still burned. The general seemed to have gone, as had everyone else except the woman who'd acted as translator. She knelt and tended his foot. He tried to move but remained bound to the chair. He wanted to wipe the sweat off his brow.

"Thanks, lady."

She did not reply.

"You do that good." The woman was bathing his foot. She could have used ice, but who finds ice in the middle of the jungle? Corrigan maybe, and where the hell was he? Instead, she used a solution made from herbs. Perhaps that would take away the pain, clean out any infection. Contardo appreciated the relief.

"You're a nice lady, lady."

Contardo did not believe this respite from torture would last. The general would be back with his swagger stick and his four goons. That he knew. *When?* That was the question. What they would have in store for him was another.

"What are the National League standings?" he asked.

She looked up. "Do not talk so much. I do not know the standings of the National League."

"So, you can talk without that Jap brass hat feeding you lines all the time."

People entered the room. Contardo saw the shadows of two men. They spoke quietly with the woman. Whatever they said, it sounded urgent. The woman responded tersely, then she brought a box and propped Contardo's foot on it. The shadows disappeared. She looked over her shoulder at the door before giving Contardo's wounds one last bath.

"I must go now." She went the way of the shadows.

Contardo did not get a good look at her. He could tell by her voice that she was young. She had healing hands. He sat alone. He wished she would come back. He would even settle for the general and his goons. He wondered how the other Rangers were doing. He was a little down because his plan hadn't worked, but his foot felt better. The woman had to be beautiful. He wondered what had happened to McLeane.

Chapter Fifteen

The Japanese woman fell in love as soon as she laid eyes on the handsome American with the lean, tough body and the square jaw. He was resting in another part of headquarters, in a larger room than the one in which she had just bathed the other American's foot. This Yank's shoulder was a mass of blood and scar tissue. He would need surgery, stitches. He had to be in incredible pain, yet he appeared quiet and in control. She went to him, and he smiled. Something happened to her. In that instant she wanted him. Perhaps too much time alone in the jungle had made her vulnerable. But no other man made her feel as he did. She hoped the guards had not noticed her weakness.

McLeane's wound looked even worse now that she was close. She called for more light, and one of the guards brought a combat lamp from another part of the room. She said something to one of the men who left and came back with a basin, a bottle of antiseptic, bandages, and sutures. Major Imamura followed her. He seemed pleased with himself. It did not bother him that he had lost every one of his men. *He had McLeane!* He felt good about himself. He made sure the woman, a crack combat nurse, understood that he wanted McLeane well cared for. He felt responsible for whatever happened to McLeane. He spoke to the woman in Japanese. When he left the room, the woman turned all of her attention to the American.

"I can only patch your arm," she said. "I cannot make permanent repair. Permanent repair will require much time and hands that know more."

"I think your hands know a lot."

"I do not know surgery. I studied only two years medicine. I am just nurse."

She has incredible eyes, McLeane thought, eyes that look right through your soul. He hoped she knew how to fix a shoulder—his shoulder. This lady looked nice, and he did not like to think that she might mess him up.

"This will hurt." She was ready to stitch him up. Her glance asked him if he was ready for the pain. "I have nothing to give you. I am sorry. I know in your country whiskey—"

"What do you know about my country and whiskey?" Even in the middle of Saipan, at the height of the war, McLeane could be charmed. He wanted to know about this delightful creature who knelt before him.

"I have never been in your country, but I studied medicine in England. It is the same."

McLeane didn't have the heart to explain the differences.

"Do what you have to do."

She swabbed the gaping laceration with a liquid that did not deaden the sensation, and made her first stitch. McLeane flinched. She stopped.

"That's O.K.," he said.

"There will be many moments like this. I must stitch deep." She beckoned a guard to move in with his flashlight. She put fifty-six stitches in McLeane's shoulder, front and back. Each one hurt, but McLeane remained silent. However, his body tensed, and sweat poured from his forehead and his upper lip. The nurse swabbed him with cotton and thick pads of gauze. He looked at her with his blue eyes, said nothing; and she loved him. She loved him more than ever.

McLeane found her very pleasant, although very plain. She wore baggy clothes, and her hair was tucked under her cap. Her face never changed expression except for her eyes. She smiled with her eyes. She dressed his wound, binding the gauze tightly, then making a sling so he could carry his arm without strain.

When she finished, she looked up at the guards, said something, and they left. She waited to make sure they were gone; then she got up and checked the door. Turning, she rushed to McLeane, threw herself at him, and kissed him passionately. McLeane could not move, but this good woman's efforts on his behalf did not go unappreciated.

The door opened. When Imamura entered, the guards left. He stood over McLeane, who looked up and smiled. McLeane had been catnapping.

"Well, Major, I guess you got me."

"I guess I do." Imamura knelt down and offered McLeane a Chesterfield. McLeane could not believe how thoroughly American this Japanese officer was.

"Lousy cigarette," McLeane chided.

"But yours."

"That's how I know."

They both laughed.

"How's the arm?"

"I'll never pitch again, but I wasn't a lefty anyway."

"Tell me about Columbia."

McLeane realized Imamura knew much more about him than he knew about his captor.

"Forgive me," he extended a hand. "I'm Jinichi Imamura, Major, attached to the Eighth Combined Special Landing Force. My mission is to stop your ass."

McLeane broke up. The laughter made his shoulder hurt. They get you coming and going, he thought.

"Why do you want to know about Columbia?"

"I'm Princeton, class of '38."

"Columbia's classics department is better. Physics is red-hot. In fact, I hear rumors they're working on . . . Well, fuck rumors."

"You played football."

From Flagg's performances McLeane knew of the desperate condition of American intelligence, but he'd never believed the Japs' to be better. Since Imamura knew so much, he might have to reconsider.

"Only second string."

"You beat Stanford in the Rose Bowl. That was '34."

McLeane's respect for Japanese intelligence grew, though what good this piece of information would do anyone he had no idea.

"I was still only second string."

"Quarterback."

McLeane nodded. These guys read the papers.

"But you didn't get me down here to talk about old football games."

"Very astute, Major."

They eyed each other for a while. Rather, Imamura eyed McLeane.

"So what do you want to know?" McLeane butted out his Chesterfield. Imamura offered him another, took one himself.

"Why are you here? That's an interesting question. Another one would be: what is the American plan of attack? These are the questions that concern the High Command." He pointed vaguely behind him. "But these are not the questions which interest *me*.

"Frankly, Major, I don't want information. I just want you. I have a score to settle. You see, you wiped out my patrol taking Hill 457. I didn't like that and now I want my pound of flesh."

McLeane nodded. There was certainly no beating about the bush here. He liked that. He didn't necessarily like the probable consequences, however.

"We will have to torture some information out of you. You don't have to tell us anything terribly secret. It's all just a front so I can finally get my revenge. You understand?"

"Perfectly."

"Meanwhile, can I get you anything?" He handed his Chesterfields to McLeane. To refuse them would have been impolite. "Anything else?"

"No." McLeane looked around. "No, everything's fine. Thanks."

"Sorry about the accommodations. We do have better in Tokyo and Kyoto."

"I'll render my opinion when I get there."

On his way out Imamura stopped to give McLeane the thumbs-up sign and a good, old Western wink. Japanese intelligence had, unquestionably, done its work. Flagg could learn a lot from them.

McLeane awoke, still in his seated position, to find the guards gone and dawn breaking through the cracks in the walls of his new accommodation. The two camp lights still burned. Little had changed. The pain in his shoulder hurt more and something about the room made him uncomfortable, something he could not identify, a presence he could not see.

From the corner of his eye, out of the shadows, he saw her move toward him, the woman who had sewed his wound, tended his pain. He saw her glide in his direction, her black hair now down around her shoulders, her naked body taut, her skin shimmering in the half-light. She stood before him. Her perfect breasts, soft and inviting, were just above the level of his eyes. She dropped to her knees, leaned forward, and kissed him fully on the lips, probing his mouth with her tongue, caressing his loins. She nibbled his neck, his ear.

"You beautiful man," she whispered. "I love you."

McLeane forgot the pain in his shoulder and turned his attention to the pleasure in his groin. With this brave and lovely Japanese woman caressing him he needed relief. He tried to adjust his pants. She pushed away his hand and, pressing him against the bamboo behind, drove her tongue down his throat. She massaged his cock. McLeane could not move. His passion rose. He ached.

"I love you," she whispered again as her hand loosened his belt and opened his fly. She worked his cock, then stopped. "Do you want me bad?"

McLeane nodded.

She dropped her head. Her soft, warm mouth circled his throbbing meat. He felt her fingers on his testicles and under his ass. Her black hair bobbed. His shaft poised ready to explode. McLeane stifled a groan. The woman looked up.

"We will fuck. You will fuck me hard and good, handsome man." She smiled, stood up, and spread her legs over him.

McLeane watched as she played with herself.

"Yes, beautiful man. Yes." She threw her head back. "I will do beautiful things for you."

She lowered herself on top of him, gasping as he entered her wet softness. McLeane wanted her, wanted to grab her.

"Come on, handsome man. Come on." She rode him, slowly at first, coaxing him, then harder and more frantically. "Come on. Come on."

As she approached the height of her passion, her black hair shook from side to side. Her motions became more violent. She groaned deeply, from some inner place.

"Do me. Fuck me. Do me. Fuck me." Her right hand reached under his butt. She played with him. She threw her tits in his face. The woman had gone mad with heat. This quiet Oriental nurse had lost her inscrutability, if not her mind. In a moment she shook, shuddered, and let out a cry. McLeane thought she would bring the entire Japanese army running.

"Yes! Yes! Yes!"

McLeane exploded. He grabbed her with his good arm. They writhed together, then were silent and still.

Chapter Sixteen

The Rangers had not spoken for some time. Instead, they lay awake in their prison pen unable to sleep, occasionally looking up at the rifles pointed at them, wondering how Contardo was doing, wondering what to do next.

"What do you think they're doing to him?" O'Connor asked finally.

"What do you mean what are they doing to him?" Heinman said. "He's probably already been taken to headquarters and by now he has them all pinned to the wall."

"With his nose." Wilkins sounded as though he were talking to himself.

"Do you think any of these Nippos understand English?" O'Connor seemed concerned. Heinman wondered if any of the *Rangers* understood English, but he didn't want to press the point. He said something to their guards in Japanese. One guard shook his rifle up and down and rattled away. Like some kind of fucking squirrel, Wilkins thought.

"What'd he say?"

"He says the Japanese will win the war for the glory of the Emperor."

"What did you ask him?"

"I asked him if he understood English."

"Does he understand Japanese?" Wilkins seemed confused.

"We should fuck these guys and get our guinea brother out of there." O'Connor said.

The same Jap who had spoken before told him to shut up.

They said no more, but they thought about McLeane. By now he must have realized that they had been captured. They could not help but feel sheepish. Sooner or later he would save their asses. He usually did. But they wanted to save their own.

"How we going to do this?" Wilkins blurted out. The talkative Jap shook a rifle barrel in front of Wilkins's nose.

"Tell that asshole he's got the wrong fucking nose, Adolph."

"You tell him."

"This ain't no time for arguing." O'Connor, of all people, had a need to keep the peace. The Jap kept at it with his rifle barrel, kept at it and kept chattering away. Heinman told him to get lost. The Jap did not seem to hear.

"I'm warning him." Wilkins had a nervous edge to his voice. Neither O'Connor nor Heinman liked it.

Suddenly, Wilkins kicked out with his foot. The Jap tripped and went down. None of the Rangers

174

moved. None of the Japs fired. The Jap that went down got up slowly. Heinman sat, every muscle in his body taut. For an instant anyone could have cut the tension with a knife. Then the Jap gave Wilkins the butt of his rifle in the face. Wilkins's head snapped back. He barely blinked. Blood ran down his nose. The Jap took another look at him. He cocked his arm to hit him again. Another Jap stopped him. All three Japs just looked at Wilkins.

"Assholes." Wilkins spit the blood off his upper lip. The morning sun cast a shadow over their tiny quarters. "I'm hungry," he continued. "Ain't you fucking slant-eyed assholes going to feed us anything?"

No one answered.

O'Connor looked overhead. It would be a long day. Heinman looked at Wilkins. It would definitely be a long war.

McLeane could tell from the way light poured into his quarters that the nurse had been gone about two hours before returning, this time fully clothed. Once again she wore her hair under her cap, her fatigues tied loosely around the firm, warm body with which McLeane had just become acquainted. She did not look like the hot tigress who, with the breaking dawn, had so wantonly spent herself on his shaft. Instead, she was every bit the professional soldier, the passionless nurse. She had come to dress his wounds. He noticed that she had the rank of lieutenant.

With great care, using all her skill, she removed McLeane's bandage. He could not see the sutures. She bathed the fierce laceration with a clear solution

175

that burned. McLeane wondered why he should be given such preferential treatment. At that moment Major Imamura entered. He could ask.

"How come the? . . ." He gestured toward the nurse.

"The expert medical care or the beautiful nurse?"

"Both." He took a Chesterfield from Imamura.

"Don't worry, McLeane. In a little while you won't like the treatment you get." He smiled. "Unless, of course, you decide to help us out . . . which I seriously doubt."

He said something in Japanese to the nurse. McLeane understood that she'd been told to hurry. The nurse nodded. Imamura left. McLeane liked him even if he had gone to Princeton. Two guards came into the room.

"You must escape." She did not look at him, but busied herself with his dressing. She had just showered. In the thick, relentless jungle air her hair smelled fresh. She seemed to take an especially long time with the bandage. "Escape soon."

The words caught McLeane by surprise.

"Do not worry. The guards do not understand— either English or my hatred of torture." She leaned toward him to adjust his bandage in the back. Her breasts brushed his hand. He wanted to grab her, pull her to him, kiss her hard on the mouth, and rip away her clothes.

"We can do that later," she said, sensing his need. "Now I must go. Your men need help."

McLeane watched her get up and silently leave, without nodding to the guards. He wondered what

176

she had in mind, and if he could trust her.

Two explosions, one right after the other, rocked the entire compound minutes after Imamura and the officer who looked like a general entered McLeane's room. The officer had little chance to slap his swagger stick against his palm. He did get a chance to walk up and down and to ask McLeane why he was there and when the Americans would attack. He also made some grand statements: "We know who you are" and "The Emperor will win." But he never really got to know McLeane, never retrieved any information from him, before the blasts. The Japs were thrown back hard against the wall and onto the floor. "O'Connor," McLeane mumbled.

McLeane, despite his exhaustion and his bad arm, sprang like a panther. All the Rangers were good at capitalizing on the other guys' mistakes. Before anyone reacted, McLeane grabbed a 6.5-mm type 3 submachine gun from one of the guards and began spraying bullets in a semicircle, twice, then four times, until he'd emptied the weapon.

One guard escaped, crashing through the door without bothering to open it. The other took so many bullets in the throat that his head was held to his neck only by a thin muscle. The general sat upright where the wall met the floor, his eyes wide open, swagger stick in hand and so much lead in his chest that his blood flowed in little rivulets.

Imamura drew his automatic and was about to waste McLeane when the American flung himself across the room and, using the 6.5-mm like a bat, smashed his Jap adversary across the arm. At that exact moment, the wooden stilts supporting that end of the compound collapsed. The room tilted, hurtling McLeane and Imamura against the far wall. They vied for position with each other and with the force of gravity. Imamura managed to lower himself out a window and to drop into a clump of areca palm and dendiki. McLeane followed. He ripped the bandage from his injured arm and felt excruciating pain. Still, he must risk being maimed in order to get Imamura. He needed at least an arm and a half to take the man. In the background he could hear the sounds of heavy fighting. The Rangers flashed into his mind.

Imamura no sooner stood up than McLeane dropped him from the side with the kind of classic tackle quarterbacks are not supposed to make. Imanara went straight on to the ground—dead weight. How many times had he been brought down by some Princeton lineman? McLeane was only giving them back some of their own.

Both men were unarmed. McLeane fell on Imamura and tried to grab his throat. Imamura wrenched himself away. In a move a professional wrestler would have been proud to make, the Jap turned the tables on the American. McLeane found himself on his back, looking up at an intense yellow face. He felt the pressure of a thumb on his windpipe and the air going out of him. He wanted to render a rousing chorus of "Roar, Lion, Roar." The situation called for at least one round of the old college fight song, but he couldn't get up the breath for it.

"I'm going to miss you, McLeane." Imamura smiled at his victim, his face free of the inscrutability of the Orient. He had McLeane's ass, and he loved it—for a few seconds anyway.

With daylight fading fast, McLeane had no choice. With a superhuman effort he brought his right knee up and his arm across. He hit Imamura in the groin and behind the ear at the same time. Imamura rolled to the side, slowed by the blow to his groin. McLeane spun away and got to his feet. Imamura knelt on one knee, holding his crotch, his head down. McLeane put the toe of his boot squarely in the middle of Imamura's face. The contact was clean. He wanted to see a Jap head sailing thirty yards through the uprights for three points. Instead, Imamura fell backward, dazed. McLeane gave him another shot, with the heel this time. Imamura took it without a whimper. He tried to clear his head. McLeane wanted to clock him with a right, wanted to land a good, old Yankee cross to the jaw, just one. Imamura lay flat, unable to move.

"Go ahead," he said. A faint curl appeared on his lips. "Give me everything you've got."

McLeane hesitated, why he would never know, but in that instant Imamura hurled a rock that caught him full in the face. While McLeane stood stunned, blows came at him from all directions. He damned the mountainous terrain of Saipan and, at the same time, wondered where Imamura had learned to throw punches. Certainly not at Princeton. Japs, trained in the martial arts, never threw body shots like that. The sutures on his left arm had long since opened and he could feel blood running down his

179

side and sticking to his shirt.

Before Imamura had a chance to do much more damage McLeane landed a right cross, hard and clean, to the jaw. The Jap reeled backward. McLeane kept on top of him and connected again. McLeane's hand hurt. He hit Imamura one more time—another right cross, all three home runs. Still Imamura was not out for the count. He hit the dirt and immediately began looking for another rock. McLeane ran at him ready to kick him off the island when Imamura broke for the thick, jungle forest. McLeane did not understand. The Jap had just run away. The American stopped at the edge of the brush and foliage. Imamura had disappeared. Behind him, McLeane heard the incessant chatter of machine-gun fire. He turned to see the headquarters in flames. The Rangers had done it.

Chapter Seventeen

Like pieces of iron on a magnetic field, the Rangers came together. No matter where they were or under what conditions, they knew how to make contact. Either through instinct or training they regrouped, until all were assembled in the middle of a clearing on the edge of the compound at a safe distance from the crumbling Jap headquarters. The fighting had ended. In the jungle stillness all anyone could hear was the crackling sound of burning wood.

McLeane was the last to show up. He came through the brush upright, his strides defiant and angry. His eyes fell on Contardo and on the Japanese nurse bathing his tortured foot. She soaked the bandages with antiseptic from a large bottle. The Flatbush Kid never flinched.

"Sorry, Mac." He referred not only to his present state but also to the predicament in which the Rangers had found themselves. They had been captured.

Wilkins sat silently, cleaning a U.S. carbine. A stack of weapons lay at his side. He looked up and raised his hand to the major./

"Hello, Major." Heinman walked over and extended a warm hand. "Don't ask me how, but we did it."

O'Connor knelt facing the fiery ruin, looking up to see the results of his work and then down again to sort through his demolition equipment. His guilt over having fallen asleep resurfaced. He did not want to say anything to McLeane, but he did make a gesture. He looked in his direction and nodded.

"What's wrong with O'Connor?" McLeane asked Heinman. "And how did you do this?"

McLeane's eyes fell on Contardo again.

"And what happened to you?"

"I had this great need for a toe manicure. You know how dirty life gets in the jungle. I needed a pick-me-up, something to make me feel better after—"

"Be still." Heinman was not quite prepared for humor. "Contardo here decided he couldn't stand being pent up in—"

"Let's start from the beginning, Heinman."

McLeane was about to lose his temper.

"Yes, of course, Major."

The two men stood in the center of the clearing, circled by the Rangers and the Japanese nurse as Heinman told McLeane how O'Connor and the rest of the Rangers fell asleep and were captured, how Contardo tried to break out and got taken to the toe manicure room.

"They don't know how to do it very well."

182

"Shut up."

The fact that Contardo did not continue talking meant that his foot hurt beyond the limits of super-human endurance. McLeane walked over to get a better look at it.

Contardo's foot looked like roasted meat. It was swollen. Scabs capped the toes and there were red marks above the ankles. McLeane knew how hard his whole leg must be throbbing.

"Do you have any painkillers?" he asked the nurse.

"I ain't taking no fucking painkiller."

"He won't," the nurse said with resignation.

"They make me drowsy, and I ain't sleeping."

"Can he walk on this?" McLeane asked her. She shook her head.

"Why the fuck don't you ask me? It's my foot. Yeah, I can walk on it, run on it, hop . . ." He jumped up to demonstrate and immediately toppled over.

"Yeah, you can run. You can hop. You can shit," Wilkins called out.

"I am concerned about infection," said the nurse. McLeane's eyes dropped to the woman whose body he had enjoyed so thoroughly only hours earlier. How well the loose fatigue shirt hid her lush breasts. How well her fatigue pants covered her ample hips and soft belly. But he remembered, and he wanted her.

"He won't get an infection," McLeane said. "There's nothing rotten enough to live in his body. He kills germs. They don't kill him."

How much of that McLeane believed, he wasn't sure. But further argument with Contardo would go nowhere. He did not want to make matters worse. Contardo struggled, unaided, to a sitting position in front of the nurse. He put his foot up and let it be bathed again in a solution so strong that McLeane could smell it from eight feet away. McLeane turned to Heinman.

"Then what happened?"

"I don't know what happened with Contardo. You'll have to ask him that. I can only say that after awhile we heard scuffling outside our stockade. Then this lady entered." He pointed to the nurse. "She had a stack of our own weapons waiting for us, the ones the Japs took when they captured us. That included O'Connor's fireworks. She told us where Contardo was and said that you were nearby. We got Contardo out, killed a few of the enemy on the way, then let O'Connor blow everything."

He paused.

"We imagined you could take care of yourself."

Both men smiled.

"Do you want to hear about the torture room?"

"Some other time." McLeane could not keep his eyes off the nurse.

"How is your shoulder?" she asked, looking up at him.

"I think it needs attention."

McLeane had removed himself to another part of the jungle, not far from what used to be Jap headquarters, but far enough from his men. They had only completed half the mission. By all accounts Jap guerrillas were bunkered between them and the

American forces to the south. They had to go in and remove some of those guys. Yet, surprisingly, he did not hear friendly artillery, and the jungle was too still to suit him.

The men were in reasonably good shape. He'd left them comfortable, if not happy. Except for Contardo, they were all in one piece, and even half a Contardo equaled a detail of ordinary killers. He wondered about getting off the island. Hooking up with Corrigan had always been problematic. He lit a Chesterfield. The Japanese nurse remained in the back of his mind. They could not stay in the jungle forever. His kind of commando operation depended on hitting and running.

His body tensed.

Someone was approaching from behind him.

He spun around,

Before him stood the nurse, her hair loose over her shoulders, her fatigue shirt open in front, exposing a hint of the breasts he remembered so well. Indeed, the shirt was all she was wearing; she had removed her pants. Barefooted, she came to him and threw her arms around him.

He backed up and leaned against a lone banyan tree, holding her close to the strong side of his body and kissing her hard. Her tongue ravaged his mouth. An experienced hand felt his thigh, his groin, rubbed his aching passion up and down. She reached for his belt and in two swift moves his throbbing cock was free.

The nurse dropped to her knees and McLeane felt her soft, warm lips on his member. He looked down. Her head bobbed in and out. He put a gentle hand on her ebony hair, then pulled it tight. She looked up and smiled. All the time her hand worked. McLeane suppressed a groan. Her eyes found his again.

"I love you," she said without losing the rhythm.

McLeane wished she didn't, but it was too late to change that.

"Fuck me." She spoke softly. Her lips were easy to read. "Fuck me. Fuck me."

Her eyes glazed. She rocked with the movement of her hand. Her free hand moved between her thighs. She sucked in air as she touched herself. She stared straight at McLeane as she stimulated herself. A smile unfurled.

She stopped, hesitated an instant, then threw herself in front of him on all fours and slowly raised her ass in the air, waving it shamelessly before his face.

McLeane dropped to his knees and mounted her from behind.

She bit her arm to keep from crying out. Waves of ecstasy ripped through her body. Tears clouded her eyes. McLeane drove into her with even strokes.

"Take me. Take me. Take me!" Her words came in a desperate whisper. McLeane took her.

"Yes. Yes." She moved back against him, in rhythm, her perfect, yellow ass slapping his belly. He reached around with his good arm and pressed a nipple between his thumb and index finger. She shuddered.

"I'm going to again. I'm going to . . ." She never finished. Instead her whole body shook. "Yes, yes."

McLeane did not slack off, but drove deeper, harder. She became frenzied. Lifting her head, she shook it from side to side. He gave a final thrust and exploded.

They held each other for one frozen moment, then collapsed. McLeane rolled onto his good side on the soft jungle floor. He had the distinct feeling they were being watched. His sixth sense never rested.

The woman lay next to him, naked and covered with sweat. McLeane wished he could forget about the war. He checked his carbine. He did not like being vulnerable. His eyes panned a three-quarter circle. He got up slowly and brought the woman's shirt over to her. She sat up and put it on. They did not speak. With her hair down she was very beautiful. He resisted the urge to reach over and cup her breasts before she covered them.

"You must not have much respect for me," she said.

"It's war time. We both have to get it when we can."

"You are very beautiful, Major." She buttoned her shirt incorrectly and had to begin again. "And you remind me of my husband." She looked at him with embarrassment. "I hope that does not make you feel bad."

"Not at all."

McLeane never felt comfortable making cuckolds. His eyes moved again. He wanted to find Japs and shoot them.

"He was English." The woman stood and tried to cover herself. She wanted to put her hair in a bun, but as she reached to tie it up, the shirt rode above her hips, revealing more than she wanted to show. "He was a doctor. I met him in London. I was studying to

187

be a doctor too.''

She spoke nervously. McLeane already had learned more than he wanted to know. He watched her go into the jungle and retrieve her pants. She came out the plain nurse who had tended his wounds. She walked over to him.

"My husband is dead. He died in the London bombings. He was a good man. I went home to Japan. That was a mistake. I am not proud of my people.''

Her eyes searched McLeane's face.

"You may have me whenever you have need, Major. I will do anything for you." She reached up and kissed him tenderly. McLeane put his good arm around her. They stayed that way for a while, then sat down together. She rested her head on his shoulder. Silence lay over them like a blanket.

Some yards away Major Imamura put down his field glasses. He did not smile.

A Jap whore, he thought. He would take care of her himself, later.

At the first crack of rifle fire, O'Connor opened up. All of the Rangers had been nervous about the prevailing silence. Each knew a confrontation was coming. O'Connor was the first to hear them approach. He had been sitting upright, his eyes scanning the brush in all directions, looking for trouble. When it came, he was ready. The Japs had made a semicircle around them. The Rangers had their backs to the smoldering embers of the ruined headquarters. Across the clearing, the brush no doubt hid more Japs. As O'Connor saw it, they were only slightly better off than being pinned against the ocean. He moved to his left and concentrated a spray of fire straight ahead. He heard a grunt and, in the Pacific twilight, saw an enemy soldier fall forward through the shrubbery.

"Fuckers!" He saw Contardo stand and run at the same line of brush farther up, carbine chattering. Then he watched as his lunatic comrade lobbed two grenades into the jungle.

The son-of-a-bitch is out of his mind, O'Connor thought. He's got a foot cooked like a roast, waiting to get gangrene, and he runs on it. Even more dumb, he stands up when everybody else is lying down. And nothing happens to him!

Japs flew into the air., O'Connor could not tell how many.

There is definitely no God, O'Connor decided, and savaged the bushes in front of him with more 6.5-mm shells.

Meanwhile, Wilkins had found a tree, a low-hanging areca, from which he did what he did best—sniped—firing single, long shots at unwary Japs. Part of being a world-class marksman is having eyes like a hawk. Nothing got past Wilkins. Enemy riflemen hunkered behind a tree had their glasses snapped at the bridge from a hundred yards. Wilkins hadn't chewed tobacco in months. Shooting Japs on Saipan that evening made him want to chew tobacco, and he spat a river onto the ground beneath him.

Heinman waited for the enemy to come through the gate. He wanted them hands-on. He wanted to break all their bones. The opportunity to use his black belt training had been lacking. He had a need to crack skulls. Until he got that chance, however, he stuck with firepower. He fired a few more rat-a-tats into the unknown and heard a couple of screams. A lot of them must be out there, he thought, and he continued to fire with everything he had.

Chapter Eighteen

McLeane heard the carbines and the Jap machine guns at the exact moment they started up, the two grenades the second they blew; and he knew the battle had begun again. The nurse had fallen asleep in his arms. He laid her gently on the ground. There, she pulled her legs to her chest and, with her eyes closed, reached out for McLeane. He covered her with broad areca palms and maomori, and she slept on as McLeane harnessed his tools of war and turned to destroy the enemy.

He did not get far.

The half-dozen Japanese soldiers who had surrounded him quietly emerged from the bushes. They stood silent and motionless, their weapons pointed straight at him.

This move had nothing to do with winning anything for the Emperor, McLeane thought, putting down his gear. Someone wanted his Yankee ass, and he would bet his major's paycheck complete with Ranger and combat differential that the someone was Imamura. Otherwise, these sons of Hirohito would have sent all his parts flying back to Tokyo before he even knew what hit him.

Two soldiers cautiously approached McLeane while the other four kept their eyes and their carbines glued on him. McLeane waited for them to get closer. On the one hand, he was exhausted. On the other, he had had it with Saipan and Imamura. His arms hung loose. His weight was balanced delicately on the balls of his feet. He was looking ahead, but could see quite well peripherally. He kept his breathing shallow. The nurse slept, camouflaged, behind him. He figured they wanted her too.

When he charged, they went reeling. Ignoring the pain in his left shoulder, he ripped the 97s out of their hands and swung one in an arc, smashing them both unconscious. Then he hit the ground on his back and, spinning a full circle, opened fire. The Jap soldiers, stunned by what they saw, hesitated an instant. In that instant they died.

Unbelievable, Imamura thought, watching from the bushes. The man is unbelievable. He wanted a rematch and charged up to McLeane whose submachine gun had run out of ammo.

Imamura's appearance came as no surprise to McLeane.

"Hi," he said looking up at his adversary and catching his breath.

"Major."

"Didn't I just see you a couple of hours ago?"

"Back there." Imamura pointed toward the ruined

headquarters building. "We had a little misunder-standing."

"Actually, I thought we understood each other pretty well."

"Just another little Ivy League rivalry." With that Imamura threw himself on top of McLeane. The two men rolled around struggling for position.

The Japanese commando leader got the advantage. With his hands around McLeane's throat he worked at choking the life out of the Yank hero. McLeane looked into Imamura's face and saw the damage he had done earlier—the bruised cheek bones, the broken nose, the mouse over the left eye.

Some guys never learn, he thought and kicked the Jap hard enough to hurt all his relatives back in Tokyo. Imamura let out a yell the Emperor himself must have heard. But he didn't move. McLeane kicked him harder. This time Imamura went flying.

He recovered before McLeane had a chance to nail him. The two men circled each other. Their confron-tation had become more than a war effort. Their egos were involved. Each had to prove something to him-self.

Even though he moved well, McLeane knew Imamura was hurt. They went at each other like sumo wrestlers, grabbing low, reaching high. Then Imamura got him again. The wear and tear had already begun to affect McLeane's bad shoulder when Imamura pulled him by the left arm in a judo ploy that sent the American sailing. He hit the ground on his back. The wind went out of him, and for a split second he could not see. In that moment Imamura had him. He pulled McLeane to his feet and let him have a barroom right cross. McLeane fell into a cluster of maomori on the edge of the clearing. Imamura pulled him up and waffled him again.

"You think I don't know how to fight like a cowboy," Imamura said smiling. "I'm going to make you look worse than I do."

He let McLeane have another haymaker. Then he picked McLeane up off the ground and flipped him one more time. McLeane's head spun. He couldn't catch his breath. Blood ran from his right eye. He wiped it on the back of his hand. The sight of his own blood riled him. He whirled and stood.

Imamura decided to wait for him. This proved to be a mistake. McLeane lunged for the nimble Jap, who tumbled backward. McLeane hit him with three of the fastest rights ever thrown in or out of the ring. Imamura dropped, stunned. McLeane gave him a solid boot in the face. That one, McLeane knew, loosened a few teeth. Imamura shook his head. McLeane gave him another solid shot with his right boot.

Imamura knelt in the middle of the clearing, half-conscious. McLeane, not in great shape himself, prepared to finish him off. Then Imamura found a weapon, a Nambu pistol, dropped by one of the detail McLeane had so thoroughly destroyed.

"Don't, Major." Imamura raised the weapon. He may not have had his full powers, but the piece of iron in his hand made him feel better, evened the score.

"Stop."

The voice came from behind Imamura. Imamura lowered his pistol.

194

The voice said something in Japanese. Imamura dropped the weapon. He turned to see who spoke. The nurse had emerged from her cover of areca palm and maomori, holding a Type 97 machine gun.

She said something else in Japanese, and Imamura struggled to his feet.

"Do you want me to kill him, Major?" She addressed the question to McLeane. McLeane hesitated. Imamura did not flinch.

"No," McLeane heard himself say.

Imamura did not stir and said nothing. The nurse got up and moved to within a few feet of him. At that distance she couldn't miss. One pull of the trigger and he would be dead.

McLeane pushed Imamura to the ground on his belly, drew a thin cord from his belt, and hog-tied him like a calf at a rodeo. He reached over and tore a swatch from the nurse's fatigue shirt. With that he gagged his captive. Then he dragged him over to a clump of jungle brush.

He took a look at his work. The cord was for negotiating cliffs. All the Rangers carried it. He hoped he wouldn't need it.

"Don't go anywhere," he said to Imamura.

Imamura didn't even try to speak. Would he have done the same for McLeane? He did not know.

"He is dishonored," the nurse said. "Any true Japanese son would fall on his sword rather than be tied like an animal."

"He went to Princeton," McLeane said.

Imamura was the first Jap the Rangers had let live. McLeane decided he would be the last.

"And if I catch you again, Imamura," he said.

"Don't expect the same kid-gloves treatment."

Imamura wanted a Chesterfield very badly. M[c]
Leane could not know it, but Imamura's torture ha[d]
only begun.

"Now, what comes after New Utrecht Avenue?"
Contardo had pinned one Jap through the arm with
his bayonet and he had a boot on another's neck. H[e]
was teaching them the subway stops on the Sea Beac[h]
line in Brooklyn. "Not Fort Hamilton! Not For[t]
Hamilton, asshole!"

He gave the full boot to one Jap, breaking his neck[.]

"You have another chance, flat-nose. What? What
Speak up!" The Jap muttered something in his ow[n]
tongue and Contardo wasted him with his automatic[.]
"How many times do I have to tell you? Talk Amer[-]
ican, Big A, so I can understand."

He put a couple of extra bullets in each for goo[d]
measure. The pain in his foot had given way to th[e]
pleasure he got from killing the enemy. He stoo[d]
over his work like a stork, on one leg, grinning.

O'Connor had to laugh. He'd just finished ham[-]
mering one poor slanty-eyed troope over the back o[f]
the head with a tree branch. He felt like a cave man[.]
He liked the feeling. Looking around, he notice[d]
that most of the Japs had been mopped up.

Heinman was just having fun, practicing his black[-]
belt moves on a couple of half-dead soldiers[.]
O'Connor figured he was seeing how far he coul[d]
throw them. He had to admit that Heinman was ver[y]
smooth. He didn't even seem out of breath. One Jap's[
arms clearly broken, flapped like a rag doll's as the[

196

man went sailing through the air. The other soldier had to be totally unconscious.

"Just shoot them," O'Connor called over. "It ain't nice what you're doing.'

Heinman pretended not to hear and continued throwing the two bodies around.

Wilkins climbed down from his hideaway in the areca palm, surveyed the damage, the dead bodies, and put up his weapon. He counted twenty Japs in all and that did not include the dozen or so out in the jungle that he'd shot or that Contardo had gotten with his grenades. As far as he could see, there wasn't anything more to shoot. The thought made him a little unhappy. He stood and watched Heinman for a while. When one Jap finally showed no signs of life at all, Heinman shot the other one.

The Rangers all took a deep breath.

"When are they going to send us troops worthy of our mettle?" Heinman wanted to know.

"What metal?" Contardo always had a need to pursue truth. "Metal is metal."

"Forget it." Heinman was not in the mood for semantics.

For some time no one said anything. O'Connor finally broke the silence.

"Where's the Old Man?"

"Wherever the nurse is." Contardo did not miss much.

"How does he always come up with broads?" O'Connor shook his head.

"He's prettier than we are," Contardo left his perch, hobbled over to a tree, and eased himself to the ground, making his first concession to being human.

"Well, that's not quite true."

Everyone waited to learn why that should not be quite true.

"So why isn't it quite true?" O'Connor asked.

"He's prettier than *you* are."

"What's that mean?"

"It means," Heinman said, "that he—Contardo—is at least as pretty as the Old Man."

"Want to say that again?" Wilkins piped up.

"Yeah, I am the most beautiful thing on earth." Contardo struck a pose which gave a full view of his nose.

"Very nice." Contardo recognized the voice. "Having your picture taken?"

McLeane stood at the edge of the clearing, the nurse at his side. Contardo refused to be embarrassed. The nurse immediately went to tend his foot.

"He's showing us how beautiful he is," Heinman volunteered.

McLeane let that one go.

"You guys all right?"

"Yes, sir." Their answer came in unison. McLeane took a look around. They seemed to have done a pretty thorough job. He noticed how young the troops had been. The Japs sent over kids.

"How's the foot?"

"Fine, sir. Just fine."

"It is not so good, Major." The nurse spoke matter-of-factly as she changed the bandage. She rummaged through her bag of supplies and removed a small vial. She also took out a hypo. "I have enough serum here for a shot and a half. He must have one. I am worried about infection."

"You ain't sticking me with that shit."

Suddenly, all the Rangers lit up. Contardo was afraid of needles. He could face a whole army of Jap commandos without sweating. But standing on a ladder or taking a needle terrified him. His face had a worried look.

"Oh, yes we are." For the Rangers this very moment could prove the high point of the war. Heinman said it again. "Oh, yes we are." In no time they had converged on their favorite Brooklyn Dodger fan.

"O.K., nursie," O'Connor asked, "where does he get it?"

They knew it would take all of them to keep him constrained.

"Get off me, you cocksuckers."

"If I can have his arm . . ."

"His arm?" O'Connor was disappointed. "His ass. We want his ass."

"Or shoot him in the nose," Heinman suggested. "He'll never feel a thing."

O'Connor and Heinman each had an arm in a hammer lock. Wilkins held on to Contardo's healthy foot. The bad foot he could barely move, despite his bravado.

"On three," O'Connor already had made plans.

On three, they flipped Contardo onto his stomach.

"We forgot to take his pants off," Wilkins noticed.

"Don't worry." Heinman pulled his knife and deftly slit Contardo's pants.

"What the fuck are you doing? I got to fight a fucking war. You guys fucked up my clothes."

"Take the word 'fuck' out of his vocabulary and he would have nothing to say," Heinman said.

"Hold still, please."

"Major, do you want to sit on his head?" Hein man asked.

"The suggestion has some appeal, but I'll let thi opportunity pass, thanks."

"I'll get everyone of you pricks."

The needle went in like a dart in cork.

"I'll get everyone of you rotten—"

"Shut up and take it like a man." O'Connor coul not remember when he had enjoyed himself so much

"Is he crying?" Wilkins asked from his duty sta tion at Contardo's feet.

"I'll make you cry, you fucking hillbilly."

Before long, however, Contardo calmed down an the Rangers settled in as night came over Saipan. Th nurse tended McLeane's left shoulder.

"There's nothing you can do," he grumbled. He had learned to live with the pain. He had learned to anticipate the sluggishness in his reactions. He had not learned to like other people fussing over him. "Just leave it alone."

She dabbed him with a fierce antiseptic, then swabbed the wound that had been opened more times than he could remember.

"Do not move," she told him. McLeane resigned himself to the attention. She wanted to tape his arm to his side.

"I can't fight like that."

She put away her medical supplies.

"Thanks," he said.

"I love you," came her reply. She kissed his shoulder and went to the far corner of the clearing where she made a bed of areca palm.

McLeane checked his watch. The Rangers had more work to do. They could sleep only a few hours. Light would come early. Meanwhile he would stand guard. He pulled his aching body to full stature, secured a couple of grenades, grabbed a handful of ammo for his bandoleer and, with his carbine hanging from his arm, walked the perimeter of the clearing. Any Jap out there would be in very serious trouble.

The darkest part of a summer night is short in the Pacific. It lasts three hours on both sides of midnight. At the blackest moment, McLeane heard a sound. Someone was out there. He looked down to see O'Connor, eyes wide, staring into the jungle. It could only be one person. They could tell from the kind of noise and the background silence. Maybe Imamura was out there waiting for them. They heard the sound again. McLeane and O'Connor looked at each other. Something about that sound wasn't quite right.

American shells dropped somewhere behind them. The shelling had started a couple of hours earlier. This was the first sign the Rangers had had that someone else on Saipan might be on their side.

Suddenly, a barrage of bullets went flying over the clearing. By now all the Rangers were awake. Everyone of them lay still, eyes nailed to the half-lit jungle. Another series of shots flew over their heads.

"That cocksucker," O'Connor muttered.

Wilkins rolled on his side and went back to sleep. Heinman just shook his head.

"Stupid asshole," Contardo spat out.

"Let him have his fun," McLeane said.

A few more shots rang out. The Rangers, except for Wilkins, waited. After a while, they could not even hear a rustle.

He's good, McLeane thought. He is really good.

They all sat down and appeared as casual as possible. When he finally came bounding through the brush, the Rangers were not surprised. He stood in the middle of the clearing. No one even looked up. Then he dropped his combat posture and let his gun hang loose.

"O.K., I get it," he said. "Play cool."

"Oh," said O'Connor in mock surprise. "We have a visitor."

"We do," Heinman confirmed, his attention fixed on a jungle flower he could hardly see and could not identify.

"Very funny. Very funny," Corrigan said, dropping his gear by an empty banyan and sitting down.

"He talks funny," said Contardo. "Maybe we should shoot him."

McLeane, who had been watching from the shadows, moved, hand extended, to meet his old friend.

"Good to see you, Corrigan."

"Fuck you, too." The Aussie pilot would not be comforted.

"Where are we parked?"

"The other side of the island." Corrigan tilted his head to the west.

"What was it like getting through?"

"A bitch, if you want to know. But, being who and

what I am, I made the trip without difficulty. You probably had more trouble, you being who you are."

"I always did admire modesty," McLeane said.

"Prick," Contardo mumbled from the other side of he clearing.

"How did you know it was me?" Corrigan asked.

"Your Owen."

Corrigan frowned and looked down at the horn-shaped weapon.

"There's only one of those in this jungle."

If the Rangers could have seen his face, Corrigan would have looked as though he'd been betrayed. He patted his submachine gun and set it behind him. Everyone nestled in for another hour or two. The nurse came from out of the jungle and settled her head against McLeane's shoulder. McLeane held his carbine close, put one hand on her breast, and kept both eyes glued to the undergrowth.

Chapter Nineteen

It was like old times. The Rangers moved out fresh after two hours rest, with McLeane in the lead and Corrigan, grumbling, at his side. The dawn light showered the jungle. The going was easy despite Contardo's bad foot. He never pampered himself.

"Leave me the fuck alone," he said whenever anyone tried to lend a hand. He took bold strides under his own power, walking directly on the foot that caused him excruciating pain. The nurse kept close to McLeane and held a Jap Type 97. Her eyes darted around the brush.

The regular American troops had come much closer since McLeane first heard the shelling. Now he could hear small-arms fire in the distance. He noted a bazooka about two miles away.

As the terrain turned rocky occasionally a Jap would emerge from a cave or from behind a rock. The Rangers wasted each one without so much as taking cover. Once, a half-dozen scraggly guerrillas converged on the band of Americans, dropping from trees and stony crags. Wilkins caught one in the air before the man hit the ground. He popped him with one shot and watched a piece of his target's skull fly off. Contardo's carbine jammed as three Japs rushed him. McLeane took them out. The other two Japs put their hands in the air. Corrigan shot them.

"I thought this was going to be hard," said Heinman, who didn't get into the action at all. "Flagg fucked up again."

Another time, O'Connor blew an entire hillside in a matter of minutes when the Rangers came upon one of the pockets of resistance Flagg had warned them about. Jap fire seemed to come from everywhere, but no one could see the enemy. The Rangers got down on their stomachs, something they had not done for a while. McLeane waved for O'Connor. The burly Irishman from Chicago moved quickly and easily to his commanding officer.

"There's a hill ahead of us." McLeane needed to say nothing more. O'Connor had been carrying around more dynamite than he could use anyway. "Do you want help?" McLeane asked.

"The only help I want is for everybody to stay out of my way." O'Connor disappeared into the brush. Ten minutes later a small corner of Saipan went straight up into the air. Minutes after, O'Connor reappeared.

"You should have seen them Japs. They howled like a bunch of chickens. There was a lot of them in there." He stood up, a grin on his face that went from ear to ear. "You can all get up now. O'Connor did the

206

job. There ain't nothing around here with slanty eyes."

The presence of the Japanese nurse did not occur to him, but if it had, he probably would not have kept his mouth shut anyway.

However, the Rangers were feeling their oats a little too soon. Seventy-two hours before, the Japanese had held Saipan. Even if they'd wanted to hand it over to the Yanks, and they hadn't, it would have taken awhile to get their army moved out. Meanwhile, the Japs were fighting like fanatics. Those who remained alive fought a suicidal war. Before long, the Rangers ran into kamikazes on the ground.

The noon sun beat down on Saipan. The terrain now provided little cover, and the Rangers were sweating. They had all but forgotten about the enemy until rifle and machine-gun fire sounded from the other side of the rise ahead of them. The Rangers froze and listened.

"Ain't some of them ours?" Wilkins asked.

"Someone out there has an M-7," said Heinman, noting the unmistakable sound of the grenade launcher. "Someone also has a Johnson semiautomatic."

"Stay here." McLeane climbed over the rise and disappeared. Less than a minute later he returned. "A platoon of Japs have a squad of Americans trapped. Our guys are up against a hillside, and the Japs have their backs to us."

"I could have told you that." Corrigan felt left out of the action.

"What do we do?" Contardo hadn't killed anyone in over an hour.

McLeane's plan called for drawing the Japs away from the trapped Americans, while keeping the Rangers own fire from threatening the Yanks. To do this, he made himself a decoy. With two grenades in hand he charged the Japs from behind and let fly. The first grenade got the enemy's attention. The second scored on a machine-gun nest. Not to be outdone, Corrigan followed suit, but by the time he did, the Japs had turned their weapons away from the pinned-down Yanks and onto the horizon beyond which the Rangers hid. Corrigan barely got away with his scalp.

"You are fucking dumb, Corrigan." Contardo shook his head.

"*Captain* Corrigan to you." Corrigan's move had left him frustrated.

The Rangers and the Japanese nurse waited for the Japs to come over the hill, and come they did, in one fierce wave, then another, screaming fanatically.

"My Lord!" was all Heinman could say as the first line of a dozen men raced toward him, throwing grenades and howling "Banzai!"

The Rangers cut them down with a steady stream of fire at close range. But the second line was on top of the Rangers almost immediately and not all of them recovered fast enough. What followed, McLeane would say later, looked like a schoolyard fight. The men tumbled and gouged and kicked and hit. No one could get a sound footing on the rocky hill. Both sides used their weapons as clubs. Contardo, unable to stand properly, waved the stock of his carbine at a Jap attacker like an old man using a cane to ward off thieves. Heinman tried to throw a few karate chops or land a flying kick, but he kept slipping on the smooth rock surface beneath him. McLeane stood on whatever firm ground he could find and, disregarding the bullets flying in his direction, slugged any Japs who came within reach. The Rangers finally seemed to be making progress when, suddenly, the Japanese nurse called out.

"Oh, please no!"

A Japanese soldier raced over the hill, toward them, like a drunk or a lunatic. Several feet away from them he tripped over a corpse and flew through the air. In a blinding flash he literally blew apart, shreds of his flesh scattering to the far reaches of Saipan. He had been a human bomb, carrying a land mine and a blast charge on his waist but, like the Emperor's plans for world conquest, this plan, too, was aborted. The Rangers returned to work, easily destroying the few Japs who remained alive.

Exercising none of the caution which made him the best Ranger commander in the Marines, McLeane walked to the top of the hill and looked over. He could no longer hear the fire of the trapped Americans. Across the way he noticed them packing their gear and moving out. As Corrigan joined him on the hilltop, McLeane saw a hand wave thankfully to them. Corrigan, too, spotted the gesture through his field glasses.

"A major," was all the Aussie said.

McLeane waved back.

"I thought guerrillas were supposed to hide out in trees," Corrigan said.

"I guess sometimes they don't." McLeane lit a Chesterfield and offered one to Corrigan, who turned it down. They set out for the Catalina.

As the sun retired below the Pacific, Major Imamura stared down at the seven figures on the beach. The Catalina lay under cover. Imamura smiled. He watched Corrigan go into the plane. He knew the engines would not start. He saw the Jap whore through his field glasses. He wanted her. He had wanted her back at headquarters. She had given herself to McLeane. He couldn't blame her, but now he wanted his. He imagined the body beneath her baggy army clothes. He had known a few American women in his days at Princeton. They were larger, less fine, but very willing when they decided to be. Right now he wanted some yellow skin next to his own. He wanted to ravage the yellow bitch. He realized he was thinking like an American.

He checked his Nambu pistol, loaded the Type 97 carbine, and secured grenades and ammo to his bandoleer. In his wanderings, stalking the Rangers, he had come across a cache of Japanese arms and supplies—enough dynamite and charges to blow the island off the face of the earth. He laid mines all along the beach, pockets of explosive that would detonate at the slightest contact.

All he had to do now was wait. However, he wanted to capture the nurse. He would move around behind the Rangers. He'd noticed that she always stayed on the fringe of the group. He could kidnap her at just the right moment. The war began to look better to him.

*   *   *

The swearing coming from the cabin of the Catalina made Heinman laugh.

"He sounds worse than you, Contardo." Contardo didn't answer. His foot throbbed so badly he could hardly talk. The nurse wanted to tend it, but he pushed her away. They could torture him, but he would never tell anyone how much he hurt.

O'Connor and Wilkins stood guard at their backs. They heard friendly fire in the background, but no sounds up close. Not even the palms rustled. The ocean was calm, and they could see action in the sky farther south.

"Everyone freeze!" McLeane called out in a loud whisper. No one moved. He stared down at the beach where it met the water and gently poked the sand with the stock of his rifle. "O'Connor."

The Irishman moved over to where his commanding officer stood, and stared down at the same sand.

"Do you see what I see?"

O'Connor hunkered down, but touched nothing. Then he nodded his head. His eyes traced a line along the beach in front of the Catalina.

"How come Corrigan didn't get blown to shit?"

O'Connor just shook his head.

"He had to get through that line to get to the Catalina." McLeane and O'Connor both seemed perplexed. "Unless they're strung like Christmas tree lights and one isn't working, he should be one dead kangaroo fucker."

"What are you guys doing?" Heinman had become impatient. "May I move now?"

"Yes, but be careful."

Heinman made his way, carefully to where the other two stood.

"The Old Man found a mine string along the beach in front of the Catalina." O'Connor pointed with his carbine. The swearing from the plane got louder. McLeane feared that all the noise would attract Japs, like mosquitoes to light. O'Connor carefully dug around one mine. The nurse moved away from Contardo and the explosives, nearer to the edge of the jungle.

"You know Mac, I think you're right about the Christmas tree lights. Whoever hooked them up knew what he was doing. But it's a tricky business at best."

Corrigan got lucky. He must have crossed over a dead dynamite pocket, McLeane thought. He no sooner thought that than Corrigan emerged from the plane muttering and sputtering.

"Don't come over here," McLeane called out.

Corrigan could not believe his ears. Nobody gave orders to the bravest pilot in the skies.

"Fuck you, McLeane." He prepared to descend the plane into the water.

"Don't move, damn it! The beach is mined."

Corrigan paid no attention and dropped into the shallow Pacific. Instantly McLeane laid down a line of fire in front of him.

"I said it was mined, damn it!"

"If you're going to shoot me, son, there's better targets than my feet."

McLeane frowned. Arguing with an Aussie was pointless.

"I think I know how to do this," the Irishman said finally. "Everyone move away."

McLeane stayed by O'Connor's side holding a

small flashlight. The Irishman's big hands worked as delicately as any surgeon's as he went from mine to mine dismantling each charge. Corrigan stood screaming in the background but did not move. Everyone ignored him. Only Wilkins, farther from him than anybody, wished, softly, that he would shut up.

O'Connor worked a full half-hour without disturbance before the machine-gun fire began. First came the Japs, then Wilkins's response a split second later. The nurse screamed. Wilkins fell back. A loud groan pierced the jungle stillness, followed by a sub-human scream. Heinman ran forward. He saw a shadow plunge into the brush and heard the shrubbery shake behind someone running away. He fired into the darkness.

"Son-of-a-bitch!" Wilkins picked himself up and dusted himself off. "The prick has some pair of balls. He came right at me."

"Are you all right?" Heinman helped the nurse to her feet.

"I'm fine, thank you." She did not seem the least bit shaken.

"Did someone want you?"

"Yes."

"Who and why?"

"Major Imamura."

"O.K., Corrigan, you can move now," McLeane said. He heard the water ripple and saw the shadow of the Aussie pilot wade ashore.

"Fuck you Yank." The words had a distinct Aussie accent.

McLeane wanted to get to Eniwetok.

Chapter Twenty

The eleven hundred nautical miles southwest from Saipan to Eniwetok took more than the usual time. Because of Imamura's meddling; Corrigan had to resplice the wiring under the forward panel. The Catalina still worked, more or less. With every sputter Corrigan cursed the gods, the Japs, the universe. Otherwise, he kept his eyes on the lovely Japanese nurse who had *her* eyes on McLeane. He wondered what she might look like undressed, in something more revealing than a pair of fatigues. He imagined her breasts at rest, like jello, formed a tiny, perfect slope. He envisioned her hips as wide and fertile. He had plans for her and could not wait to land.

General Thompson, Major Flagg, and Margot, together with a handful of Seabees who just happened to be standing around in the morning sun, watched the Catalina come down and the Rangers disembark. Corrigan and the nurse were the last to wade ashore. The Aussie helped her through the water in an uncharacteristic gesture.

All the Rangers shook hands with General Thompson and Major Flagg. They abandoned the customary salute. Everyone was too tired for formalities. Margot threw her arms around McLeane and shed tears of joy.

"Oh, I love you," she whispered in his ear. She was very aware of the Japanese nurse, however. McLeane knew he would have some explaining to do.

The nurse stood alone at the edge of the water while the men got reacquainted. She, too, was very aware of Margot.

"I hate to break up this reunion," General Thompson said, "but I need a word with you, Mac."

Margot reluctantly broke her hold and the two Marines moved a bit away from the others.

"Who is the Japanese woman?" General Thompson kept his voice low.

"I don't know her name, sir, but she's one hell of a fighter."

"Is *that* what you call it now?"

"Quite seriously, Arch, that woman saved my life. She saved all our lives."

Thompson just nodded.

"I've got to treat her as a POW," he said. "You know that."

"Just treat her well. She's a good lady."

"I'll have to get the MPs . . ."

"No, Arch. Believe me, she's not going anywhere. Get one of the men to take her to some nice quarters."

Thompson looked as though he wanted to protest.

"Believe me, Arch."

Thompson walked over to the nurse, who looked a little frightened. He started talking to her in pidgion English. When she answered in near-perfect English, his face turned a deep crimson.

"Would one of you men take this woman to my quarters until I can find her a suitable place to sleep?"

All of the Seabees moved at once, but Corrigan was the first to take her arm.

"I'd be more than happy to, sir."

"But you don't know where my quarters are?"

"I'll find them," Corrigan replied, hustling the nurse toward what looked like the center of Eniwetok.

The Rangers had their wounds attended to at the field hospital by a team of Australian doctors. McLeane's shoulder was one thing. They could fix that. But when they saw Contardo's foot, they had doubts that anything could be done. When he overheard them talking about amputation, he told them where to stuff their medical degrees.

"Listen you fuckheads," Contardo said, as he sat propped up in a makeshift cot. "You ain't doing nothing to my foot except kiss it when I tell you to."

"I ain't letting no one cut me. I ain't letting no one cut me in a shithole like this. And I especially ain't letting no one cut me who talks funny like you guys do, with big words and phony accents."

The doctors were taken aback.

"He's only beginning to say what's on his mind,

sirs," said Heinman, who had come to see how his favorite Brooklynite was faring. "I know him. He has much more he wants to express."

"Yeah," said Contardo, not sure if he understood very much of what was happening except that no one was touching his foot.

The doctors, after consultation, agreed to treat him as long as possible with heavy doses of penicillin, although none of them believed that his foot would improve. Since Contardo didn't trust them, he had one of the Rangers by his bed at all times.

"Do you know what a pain in the ass you are?" O'Connor asked. He was bleary-eyed and tired and still had to baby-sit Contardo.

"Just shut up and see nobody touches my fucking foot."

Behind a wall at the back of Contardo's bed, McLeane sat on an oil drum while a doctor put stitches in the muscle of his shoulder and in the outer tissue. Even though the local anesthetic did little good, McLeane didn't so much as ask for a cigarette. Instead he talked to Thompson as Margot looked on from the other side of the tent.

"Of course it didn't go according to plan. Does anything Flagg engineered go according to plan? The headquarters got blown—largely because the Japanese nurse slipped O'Connor his C-5. We killed a few Japs whenever we had to and our boys are in there now. Saipan belongs to us. But Contardo's got a foot that makes me want to throw up when I look at it. I know you didn't ask me, but I wouldn't trade one of Contardo's toenails for ten Saipans."

Thompson could tell that McLeane was just warming up to let him have it, to tell him how incompetent Flagg was and how stupid the generals were and how sick and tired he was of going on semi-suicide missions. Thompson listened. McLeane was right on all counts, and listening was the least Thompson could do.

Finally, relieved to be able to get away, Thompson said, "Well, take care of yourself, Mac." He shook hands with the toughest, smartest Marine in the corps, nodded to Margot and to the doctor, and left.

"I'm finished," the doctor declared, stripping off his gloves. "You'll be stiff for a while and in a little pain."

"What else is new?" McLeane thought. The doctor handed him morphine tablets on his way out. As soon as he left, McLeane threw them in the garbage. For a minute he and Margot sat in silence. He knew that wouldn't last. He did not look forward to what would come.

"So?" Margot glared at him, her red hair flaming under her fatigue cap, her legs crossed, her lips tight.

"So?" McLeane repeated, knowing the question very well, understanding everything Margot meant by that one word.

"The nurse . . . if that's what she really is." She moved toward him and stood with her arms folded, an easy kick from his very vulnerable body. "She is a nurse isn't she? She did save your life, didn't she?"

"Listen, Margot." McLeane could tell from the sound of his own voice that he was going to lose this round. "She helped us. . . ."

"You made love to her, didn't you?" The edge to Margot's voice was unmistakable. "You screwed her, didn't you? Didn't you fuck her?"

McLeane remained silent, wanting neither to lie nor to incriminate himself. He only wished she would keep her voice down.

"Was she good? Did the earth move for you?"

A stab of pain shot up his shoulder. He tried not to wince.

"Don't give me that 'I'm in pain routine.'"

McLeane had always been partial to understanding women.

"You're always in pain . . . in pain or in somebody else's pants." She waited for him to respond.

"Can't say anything can you, McLeane? Can't say anything because I'm right." She leaned forward. "How many times did you have her?"

McLeane wished she would keep her voice down. Margot walked toward the exit and turned.

"See these, Major?" She opened her blouse and reached behind her back. In one smooth move two gorgeous, firm breasts jumped out. She cupped them. "See these?"

Not quite sure he got her message, she went toward him. She pushed a nipple in his mouth.

"Here taste one." She stood back from him and played with her breasts. "Remember them, Major, because you'll never see them again."

With that she closed her fatigue shirt, turned, and strode toward the exit; then she stopped. For a moment she stood with her back to McLeane. He could see her shoulders shaking. Then she ran to him, tears streaming down her cheeks.

"Oh, Mac, I love you. I love you so much." She threw herself at him, grabbed him by the legs, sobbed in his lap.

"Why do you do these things to me?" she said, looking up at him, her nose running, her eyes full of water.

"War does odd things to a person," McLeane heard himself say. He could feel Margot groping for his fly. In seconds he felt her warm lips around his cock, saw her head going up and down. He took her hair with his one good hand. She moaned. Her breasts fell free. He was glad to be back.

In the general's quarters Corrigan was trying too hard to make the nurse comfortable. After escorting her there, he couldn't keep his hands off her. He put his arms around her and got her in a bear hug.

"I know you want me," he told her ear. "I know you want to feel me inside you."

She could not speak. He relaxed long enough to let one hand drop to her breast which he massaged frantically, as though he were polishing a lamp. She grunted at him and tried to free herself. He planted a kiss on her neck, then her mouth. Finally, as a last resort, she planted a knee in his most vulnerable spot. Corrigan went reeling. The nurse stood breathing hard while Corrigan suffered and cupped his balls.

"You are *not* a gentleman," she said.

"All I wanted was a little kiss," was Corrigan's feeble reply.

"I don't kiss Australians, Captain."

"Well, I'll bet you kissed McLeane. I'll bet you did a lot more for McLeane." Corrigan struggled to get up.

"Yes, I did everything for McLeane. I would do anything for him. I love him. He can do anything he wants with me. I am his."

"But didn't you see that redhead?" Corrigan made it upright.

"She is none of my business. Whatever he wants to do he may do. What I do I will only do with him."

"He won't fall in love with you." Corrigan said.

"So he doesn't love me. Maybe he will never love me. I will still be his. I will always still be his."

As Corrigan left, he tried hard to understand what had just happened. Were all women like that or only Japanese women? He had to confess a lack of expertise in the area. What did McLeane have that was so special anyway? He banged the dust out of his cap and walked back to the Catalina.

It took Major Imamura several days to get a flight from Saipan to the Japanese Sixth Army Headquarters on the Huon Peninsula. When he finally did arrive, no one welcomed him. He sat in his hut and drank sake alone. He thought of revenge.

THE BEST IN ADVENTURES FROM ZEBRA

GUNSHIPS #2: FIRE FORCE   (1159, $2.50)
by Jack Hamilton Teed
A few G.I.s, driven crazy by the war-torn hell of Vietnam, had banded into brutal killing squads who didn't care whom they shot at. Colonel John Hardin, tapped for the job of wiping out these squads, had to first forge his own command of misfits into a fighting FIRE FORCE!

GUNSHIPS #3: COBRA KILL   (1462, $2.50)
by Jack Hamilton Teed
Having taken something from the wreckage of the downed Cobra gunship, the Cong force melted back into the jungle. Colonel John Hardin was going to find out what the Cong had taken — even if it killed him!

THE BLACK EAGLES #3:
NIGHTMARE IN LAOS   (1341, $2.50)
by John Lansing
There's a hot rumor that Russians in Laos are secretly building a nuclear reactor. And the American command isn't overreacting when they order it knocked out — quietly — and fast!

THE BLACK EAGLES #4: PUNGI PATROL   (1389, $2.50)
by John Lansing
A team of specially trained East German agents — disguised as U.S. soldiers — is slaughtering helpless Vietnamese villagers to discredit America. The Black Eagles, the elite jungle fighters, have been ordered to stop the butchers before our own allies turn against us!

THE BLACK EAGLES #5:
SAIGON SLAUGTHER   (1476, $2.50)
Pulled off active operations after having been decimated by the NVA, the Eagles fight their own private war of survival in the streets of Saigon — battling the enemy assassins who've been sent to finish them off!

Available wherever paperbacks are sold, or order direct from the Publisher. Send cover price plus 50¢ per copy for mailing and handling to Zebra Books, 475 Park Avenue South, New York, N.Y. 10016. DO NOT SEND CASH.